Lore Wylie flinched when I walked into the room with Radcliffe, and pulled the covers up to her shoulders. Without a trace of makeup, she looked like an attractive ghost, instead of one of Hollywood's most highly paid actresses. But the whiteness of her face was framed on three sides by deep red hair, and that combination made her beautiful.

"This is the first time a completely strange man has ever seen me in bed." That soft slurry voice brought back memories of half a dozen movies. "It makes me feel wicked and I've never liked that feeling."

I nodded briefly and figured I should get down to business before I started acting like any other normal male confronted by such a dish. "You're in the hospital because you tried to commit suicide. The sooner you let me in on the facts, the sooner I'll be able to help you."

"Quite a few things would need to be done Mister Savage . . . my career would have to be saved, not to mention my sanity and my self-respect."

"Cut the trimmings, Lore. What made you slash your wrists?"

"Mister Savage, a good actress has to be ready to cut throats or slip into bed with a fat old producer if a good part will come her way, and I'm just not that type of girl."

"So? What's the catch?"

"Yesterday I received an envelope in the mail. It had my name and address typewritten on it, but no return address. I opened it and saw a glossy six-by-nine picture of . . . myself and another man naked together on a bed. It has to be a frame of some sort. Mister Savage, I've just never done anything like that . . . . "

# THE OUTRAGERS

## WILDSIDE PRESS

This book was published by
**Wildside Press LLC.**
www.wildsidebooks.com

# ONE

The battered old truck swayed on a turn and I said something under my breath. Extra motions made me feel impatient and uncomfortable, not only because I was in the back of the truck but because I was tied down with thick, taut hemp onto a rickety looking chair.

The two brawny men in there with me suddenly nodded at each other and moved purposefully. Bending down in front and in back of me they hefted the chair with me on it and carried it half a dozen feet to the open end of the truck.

One man asked considerately, "Okay, Mark?"

"Let's get it over with, for God's sake!"

The other man said, "Here goes, Mark!", and I was dropped, chair and all, onto the rushing stream of northbound, February morning traffic on the George Washington Bridge.

The chair held when its legs hit the steel road. A fat Buick came almost near enough to clip my toenails. Energetically I pushed myself backward. A chalk mark warned that I was getting close to the promenade and the legs of my chair made contact inevitably with the raised steel surface. That was the signal for me to push myself onto it with my burden.

In my hurry to get this over with I hit the promenade too hard and went sprawling along its toothpick-width at an off-angle. Even though a breakaway link of the protected rail as well as the grating under it shuddered and cracked into flying splinters like a wall in a nightmare — just as it had been planned to do — I was out of control as I went toppling toward the blue curtain of the Hudson River.

Quickly, and cursing myself for having forced the speed, I pushed my left arm downward to keep from hitting a submerged rock headfirst.

I became active again as soon as I felt the chilling impact of water. With each hand I pulled one knot on the rope tying me. The knots disappeared and I was wrenching off my pants, shirt and shoes as well as the special padding on my hips, knees and elbows that the clothing had covered.

With nothing on me but a bathing suit I started to surface and swam towards the sleek, heavy, black-and-white outboard that was growling in my general direction.

Harrigan, the fresh-faced young assistant director, gave a jubilant smile as he helped me out of the water and into the boat.

"That was the payoff," he said cheerfully, patting me on the back as I grabbed for a towel. "It's the best stunt you've done for us yet, Mark. It'll probably be the only first-class minute of film in the finished movie."

"It was easy to do, but a pain to rehearse," I said, pulling a blanket around me and picking up a thermos of steaming coffee. "The six hours of work with all those drivers out there was a lot worse than the stunt itself."

"You really hate the preliminaries, don't you?"

"Sure I do. In work, in sex, in whatever I'm doing, give me the main event and keep it going. Don't let me waste my time building up to it."

"Lucky you're not one of the crewmen on the picture," Harrigan grinned. "You'd have to replace the rail, the gratings, and the safety bars that we got permission to take out and use breakaways for. That'll take hours and hours, Mark."

"Well, I'll be under a shower in twenty minutes and back to Los Angeles in a day or so."

"By jet, of course. You probably wouldn't dream of going by train and seeing any part of the country."

"Not from a train. I'd go by car and stop off wherever I wanted to."

"You wouldn't want to stop off anywhere," Harrigan chuckled. "You'd ditch the car after twenty minutes and finish the trip by plane. If they ever cut you open, Mark, they'll find out that you're full of itching powder, always wanting to get things over with and get ahead to whatever's next."

"Why don't you illustrate your lectures with lantern slides?" I glanced around me. "Did you by any chance remember to bring some of the prime stuff along?"

"Whiskey? Can't you even wait till you get to a bar?"

"Uh-uh," I said. "Coffee's all right, mind you, but it doesn't get down into the guts and curl itself around your belly and squeeze. Liquor does that, and the sooner it starts the better."

7

"You're a crude cat, Savage," Harrigan told me as he pointed to the Jack Daniels on the seat next to me. "As much self-control as a hungry tiger."

I undid the cap of the bottle, took a couple of swallows, and then poured myself half a glass.

"There's a bottle of soda," Harrigan started.

"The hell with it!"

"Don't end up as a drunk, whatever you do; they live too long to suit you, brother Savage. You'll probably want to kick off at an age like thirty-five, if you even stick around that long — oh, oh! I'd better check on what the hell I'm doing here!"

I nodded and watched Harrigan fumble with the steering. Just as I was about to leave the boat at the New York side, he tipped it the wrong way and I nearly sprained an ankle.

"You should have waited a minute," he said. "If you jump out so fast, you can expect trouble."

"Kid, all I need is to finish a hard day's work and then nearly get killed because I'm in a hurry, and whoever's with me doesn't know how to do his job."

"That's not fair!"

"Well, we can *hock* it around some other time, kid. I hate to stand in a place where I'm finished for the day. See you at the box office, Harrigan."

I took a fast shower and a faster rubdown at the nearest Athletic Club, not wanting to waste much time at it and hoping I'd get to see some of New York. Whenever I'm in town I go to some section I've never seen and walk through it for half an hour or so.

An innocent looking message reached me just as I was on my way out of the club. The assistant director had written that a Miss Lynne Darling wanted to see me on private business and hoped I'd meet her in the Hotel Beckwin lobby in midtown Manhattan at half-past one this afternoon. She'd had a description of me from Harrigan, so she'd be able to pick me out with no trouble.

I shrugged my shoulders. Nothing else I could do that afternoon looked any more interesting, at least for an hour or so. I'd go and find out exactly what the woman wanted.

If I'd known what I was really getting into, I might have hopped the first jet home. Lynne Darling was going to steer me towards more tension, more plain-and-fancy trouble than even I had ever met up with in my life.

Yet it wouldn't have bothered me that this was going to be downright dangerous.

## TWO

There are names that carry suggestions with them. Take the name of Lynne Darling, for instance. It suggests a youngster just coming into her twenties, shy and demure, with wide inquiring eyes and small looking breasts that turn out to be surprisingly firm when you put a hand on them.

The Lynne Darling who clumped over to me as soon as I walked into the discreet and comfortable lobby of the Hotel Beckwin might have been a lot like that thirty years ago. She was a workworn old woman now. Those hard, reddened hands had wrung out hundreds of mops in three long decades, at least. The legs had been bent on thousands of floors. And by way of proving still further how wrong my mental picture had been, there was a red wart at the end of her pie-wedge nose.

Lynne Darling wasn't comfortable. She settled down gingerly on a dark leather chair in the northeast corner of this attractively dim-lit lobby and gazed ill-at-ease at the well-dressed men and women walking around only a few feet away. Every time her gaze shifted nervously she would milk her gloves, pulling one finger at a time.

"Mr. Savage?" she began. "Mr. Mark Savage?"

"That's right."

She looked across at as much of me as she could take in. An overstuffed chair in a hotel lobby doesn't show me at my best. I've still got the thick shoulders to help prove I played pro football not too long ago. The face is weatherbeaten winter or summer, and the crew-cut blond hair that tops my six-feet-two is as much out of place on a lobby lounger as the rest of me.

"I've heard of you, Mr. Savage," Lynne Darling said finally. She straightened up in her chair, patted a fleck of dust off the Sunday-best she was wearing, and gave her number-one-grade self-conscious smile. I guessed I'd made a conquest. "Mr. Savage, you were recommended to me by the day clerk here at the Beckwin. He told me all about you."

" 'All' takes in a lot of territory."

"He — the day clerk, that is — told me that you're a stunt man in the movies and.he said that you also work as a private detective."

"That's right."

"It seems like such a strange combination, doesn't it?" she asked me, embarrassed. "I mean, being a stunt man and private detective, both."

"Actually it worked out that way on account of something that went wrong years ago. I was stunting in a crime picture and during a fight with the hero I was supposed to pick up a breakaway chair that wouldn't do any harm after coming apart on contact, and smash it over the hero's head. For some crazy reason, though, a prop man had put a real chair on the scene by mistake. The result was that I nearly brained an actor who was worth millions. It's a miracle he survived that particular bonehead play with nothing worse than a mild concussion."

"My goodness!"

"The prop man was fired for it, of course, and the studio was so sore about what had happened that they not only dropped me off that particular picture, but had me blacklisted through the industry. For a while, I didn't think I'd get more stunt work anywhere. I figured I was finished in the business."

"Oh, I see, Mr. Savage," Lynne Darling nodded. "So you became a private detective."

"There was a friend who offered to get me a license in California and I took it on," I said. "Influence in New York is what got me a license in this state, too. I've always had contacts and most of the studio people trust me, so I've done some jobs for them between stunting assignments. (Another friend of mine got me off the blacklist later on, too, by the way.) The private investigator work is just a form of insurance for me, Miss Darling. I don't generally handle it unless there's a slow period on the stunting."

"Thank you very much for explaining it to me," Lynne Darling smiled. "I was told that you're very dependable and can be trusted. You aren't one of those cheap, greasy, private detectives a person keeps hearing about. You're different, just like the clerk said."

"I'm glad you think so, too."

I tapped my fingers against each other and looked for a while at the slowly moving minute hand of the watch I wore. Lynne Darling, her hands folded tightly, flinched at those first signs of my chronic restless impatience and cleared her throat.

"Mr. Savage, you're very influential with people from Hollywood and that's why — well, not that I blame a man for making a living by his contacts, if only he's honest about it. As long as nobody behaves like you're a thief, it's perfectly all right."

Lynne Darling pulled out a handkerchief that had been stained gray with recent tears and dabbed it against the corners of her red-rimmed eyes. She drew a deep quivery breath.

"Tell me what it's about, Lynne," I said softly, figuring that she was ready for a little direct pressure now.

She sobbed quietly. It took me some extra time to soothe her down, but she got on to the track finally. She said she worked as a chambermaid at the Hotel Beckwin. It wasn't the best job in the world, but there was no help for that. Not everybody can go to offices and handle typewriters, or tinker around in laboratories with those terrible bombs. A woman does the things she can.

By and large, Lynne Darling was happy. The work that she did brought her into contact with movie actors and actresses. A lot of them knew her and liked her. Many a star had talked to Lynne about love affairs and suchlike things. Lynne must have felt sometimes that she was part of show biz. Pride rang in her voice when she talked about it.

"And then this morning," she told me, "the trouble happened. It was this way. At about eleven o'clock I knocked on the door of the penthouse because I wanted to find out if anybody was there before I went in to clean up. I sure didn't want to disturb Miss Wylie."

"Who?"

"Lore Wylie, the actress." Lynne looked keenly at me. "Sure you know who she is?"

I'd never met her, but the name did ring a bell. Lore Wylie was a nicely stacked redhead who played wholesome girl parts as if she was living them. She always looked convinced that she was pure-minded and sweet. Such parts came alive in her hands for that particular reason, and she seemed to be doing them with a naturalness that made her even more attractive to the fans who enjoyed watching her.

"Miss Wylie's a very fine girl," Lynne went on. "A good tipper and friendly. Often she asks me how I feel in the morning and all that. A lot of people don't remember those little things."

"When the revolution comes," I said with solemn irritation, "that point will be noted in her favor before she's shot."

"Please don't make jokes about any harm happening to the poor girl," Lynne scolded gently. "It's already come to her."

"What was it, exactly?"

"Well, I knocked on the door and there was no answer, like I said. So I used my key and went in. That's when I saw the poor child. She was lying on the floor in the bathroom. There was a razor blade next to her. The girl had slashed her wrists. Blood was coming out of her, almost like water out of Niagara Falls. It was dreadful, terrible."

"And then you called for help, I suppose?"

"Indeed I did. What kind of a woman is it that

14

would let such a sweet and famous girl, an actress like that, bleed to death? The hotel doctor came up and took care of her, but he said she had to be taken to a private hospital. That was arranged, and then her manager was called in."

"So?"

"Miss Wylie's manager is a fellow named Harry Radfield." Lynne made a sour face. "One of those pushy and disagreeable men who tries to look important and always ends up by passing the buck. He lives off famous people, but he couldn't be famous himself if his life depended on it."

"Uh-huh. Did this guy Radfield do anything that was extra rough?"

"Do? Why, he behaved as if I was his worst enemy. He made me swear that I wouldn't tell any newspapers what had happened — as if I would want to embarrass anybody like Miss Wylie. Then he insisted that I stay in the apartment while he looked all around it, even in the wastebasket. Then he said he wanted me searched. Even after a woman friend of his came up and did it and found nothing on me that meant anything, Radfield had the gall to insist I was a thief."

"I suppose he couldn't prove it."

"Of course not! I wouldn't take a dollar if my life depended on it, not a single dollar. Why should I want to lose the job that brings me in close touch with so many famous people? I'd rather lose an arm or a leg."

I kept to the point. "What did this fellow Radfield accuse you of having stolen?"

"Ah, that's what I can't understand. That's what puzzles me." She squeezed her coarse hands

15

together as if she was trying not to reach the limit of her patience. "If it had been anything important like a diamond, then I would realize why he'd be upset. But this — why it's monstrous."

"What was it?"

"A picture, that's what. Not even a painting, Mr. Savage, just a common photograph. Would you believe it? That man had the nerve to carry on in such a way about a measly picture. Why, I'd cheerfully give that swine all the pretty pictures he wants if he didn't claim I had stolen this one that belongs to Miss Wylie."

"What was it a picture of?"

"He wouldn't say, except that *I* knew what it was." Lynne brushed tears out of the corners of her eyes again. "I didn't have the slightest idea, I give you my word as an honest woman. I still don't know what he was talking about, or why a photograph should have been so important to anybody on earth."

"Did this fellow Radfield make an official complaint against you?"

"Not yet, but he says he will. He swears he'll complain to my supervisor at the hotel if I don't return that picture before the day is out. And I'll be in bad trouble, Mr. Savage. How can I possibly prove I didn't steal a photograph? That's why I came to you, so you can do something for me."

I nearly smiled. Lynne's problem didn't really amount to much. A few sharp words with this Radfield, and he'd see the light. No matter how much importance he was putting on a photograph, he wouldn't want to take chances on a lawsuit for

16

defamation of character. Lynne would probably be out of this jam in less time that it'd take her to ask for an autograph.

But there was a lot more to it than that. A movie actress was obviously up to her pretty neck in some sort of trouble. And it wasn't likely to be the kind that would make head-shrinkers rub their hands with joy. Everything I'd ever heard about Lore Wylie hinted that she was too direct and had too much common sense to get jammed up like that.

So it was something else, and Lore Wylie needed a different type of operator to help her out. It would have to be a guy who didn't drop his teeth every time he smiled and who had enough connections in this town to grease the path for himself. A sharp apple. Probably a guy who had already helped other people from Hollywood when they got into jams. In fact, me. It seemed that I met each and every test squarely. But I'd have to finish this business with the maid, first.

"All right, Miss Darling," I said. "I'll be glad to look into it for you if you want me to. A little talk between Radfield and me ought to make all the difference."

"I'm sure it will. As a Christian woman I don't like violence or threats, but there are times when they seem to be necessary, more's the pity."

She hesitated before reaching into a black alligator purse and slowly drawing out a cowhide wallet. She picked a folded twenty dollar bill out of the cash compartment, then glanced up at me. Two quavers of calculation stretched the corners of her lips and vanished like waves on a carmine shore. With the bill held between thumb and forefinger she snapped the wallet shut and dropped it back into her heavy pocketbook.

"Do you think this will be enough for one afternoon's work for somebody like you?"

She pushed it at me with the unmistakable proud vehemence of a woman who has nothing but contempt for any charity levelled at her. For a split second I hesitated to take what would seem to her like such a generous fee made up of money that had been painfully earned. It took me a little extra time to decide unwillingly that the only gallant and gentlemanlike thing to do in this set-up was to take the money with thanks.

"That'll be fine," I said, pocketing it. "There won't be any expenses for me."

"If anything comes up that will add to the fee, Mr. Savage, don't hesitate." She looked down shyly. "If I should have to borrow a few dollars, God forbid, you'd be surprised to know some of the big names I could borrow from."

"I'll do the best possible job," I said quickly, starting to get up. "Everything will be taken care of."

"Oh, Mr. Savage, shouldn't I be given a receipt?"

"If you insist on it." I scrawled an acknowledgement on a piece of paper from a pocket pad. Lynne glanced at it without trying to decipher a word, then folded it gently and warmed it in her hands.

"How soon do you think you'll have time to give me a report?" she asked meekly.

"Today, of course. The sooner the better."

"I quit work at six, so if you could manage it

before that I'd be very much obliged. Imagine a man as busy as you are, Mr. Savage, taking time to help me!"

I stood up in one movement and smiled at the celebrity-struck old woman, then stalked out of the lobby as fast as I could.

## THREE

It was half-past one by my Gruen, so I spared a few minutes for two phone calls.

First, I made one of my five-times-daily calls to the apartment I had rented in the city. Nobody would answer, but that doesn't mean thère'd be no reaction. My dog, who has to stay home when I'm working, generally capers around excitedly as a phone rings, and those little calls give her some badly needed exercise. I own a collie bitch that some of the neighbor kids in the Hollywood Hills stubbornly call Rex. That's the only name she answers to, so it has stuck.

After letting the phone ring five or six times, I figured I had toned up Rexie's nervous system enough for one day, and put a business call through. Buzz Brennan was over at the *Dispatch* office, for once. He makes his living as a gossip columnist with the job of telling indirectly who is sleeping with whom. To disguise it he writes breezily about "dates" among celebrities. His specialty is what you might call submerged news.

"This is Mark Savage," I said. "I need some information."

"To hell with you, stunt man," Buzz said affably. "But I like the approach: subtle as usual. Is this about some new broad you're gunning for?"

"No, I want to know something about a personal friend of mine," I said with unusual carefulness. "Whatever you can tell me about Lore Wylie being in the hospital."

"If you're gunning for Lore Wylie, even a makeout artist like you will have it rough. A cute, five-nine redhead who won't get closer to a man than fishpole distance makes it rough for anybody. The only exceptions she makes are for kissing scenes in her pictures. She may not be frigid, but she's the closest thing to it that I've ever heard of. I don't think she ever kissed a man till she was twenty-one. That's practically what you'd expect, considering the wholesome-girl parts she plays."

"But what do you know about her being in the hospital right now?"

"According to my column this morning, stunt man, Lore is in the Dutch County Hospital and suffering from a gastric upset. But that's only what the official handout says and there could be something else wrong with her. I'd figure she wanted an abortion if it was anybody else, but not with that one it isn't."

"I'll look at Lore's shape pretty carefully when I visit her."

"She probably won't let you."

"I'll pull the covers right off her, then."

"You might do it at that." Buzz chuckled. "Well, keep me in mind if you get hold of any legitimate hot news, Mark. And when I say hot, I don't mean hot-sizzling; I mean hot-filthy. Me and my dear little readers are always panting to get the latest filthy inside news."

"If there's anything I can tell you, Buzz, I'll pass

it along good and quick."

"You forgot to thank me," Buzz said dryly, "for as much as I did help you."

"To do what? Oh. Oh yes, thanks, Buzz."

I hung up sadly. Buzz was a bright guy who had nothing but contempt for the people who lapped up those columns he wrote. I don't know if it had ever occurred to Buzz that catering to people he called "Hard-up bastards" or "out-and-out perverts" made him practically a pimp himself.

A cab took me to the Dutch County Hospital, a super-modern brick building that gleamed dully in the hazy February sun. From the outside it was mostly glass in the current style, but a few expensively weathered black bricks had been thrown in for a change of pace. The patients who were vulgar enough to kick off inside it probably went to a spotless heaven where plastic angels sang and danced all the time.

An elderly woman planted at the switchboard told me disagreeably: "No visitors for Miss Wylie . . . well, don't be so *rude* about it . . . yes, there is a Mr. Radfield visiting her, but I don't know if I can . . . yes, yes, I'll try. Go up to the visitor's room on the second floor and I'll send Mr. Radfield in if I can find him . . . yes, I'll do my best not to take too much time over it."

I rode up with a couple of ill-at-ease visitors and two doctors. A colored attendant pointed down the wide, neat hall in the direction for me to take. I walked into the visitor's room, which was empty of people except for me. I sat in one of the deep couches and dropped cigarette ashes into a narrow silver tray built chastely in a glass-covered cocktail table.

Harold Radfield came bustling in about five minutes later, rubbing his hands too hard, licking his lips and glancing at his watch. Apparently he'd been too busy to wind it; he shook his hand irritably. Five fingers raced each other through his already combed dark hair.

He was dressed as Hollywood's idea of a fourteen-carat eccentric genius: open-throat bright blue shirt, sport jacket with yellow lightning bolts designed across it, knife-creased yellow slacks, yellow stockings and royal blue shoes. He wore a monocle at the end of a long black ribbon.

"What can I do for you? I'm afraid Miss Wylie isn't seeing visitors today, not even reporters if you happen to be one."

"No, I'm not, but you'll do, Mr. Radfield. First of all, I want to talk to you about Miss Lynne Darling."

"Who?"

The chambermaid over at the Hotel Beckwin. You threatened her this morning, humiliated her in front of another woman and accused her of having stolen something. I'm surprised you don't remember it. Does that sort of thing happen every day?"

"This is ridiculous!"

"You mean you didn't do those things?"

"The woman, whatever her name is, took me too seriously, that's all. I was bothered after what had happened to Miss Wylie. Her — ah, gastric upset, and all."

"So I suppose you're not going to report Lynne Darling to her supervisor the way you said you would?"

"That's right. I've changed my mind about it, she'll be glad to hear. Tell her I said so."

"How about the property that was supposed to have been stolen, Mr. Radfield? Where id that turn up?"

"I didn't say it turned up anywhere."

"Buddy, you sure as hell know where it is, or you wouldn't be feeling so kindly about a chambermaid."

"As a matter of fact, Mis Wylie cleared up that point for me later on." Radfield screwed the monocle more tightly in front of his right eye and added, "But the big thing is that the maid, whatever her name is, won't be having any trouble. That ought to make her happy."

My lips flattened angrily. A man who could get into a frenzy and threaten a helpless old woman ought to either learn how to handle himself in a crisis or pay for his mistakes.

"Miss Darling is entitled to more than just your word," I said.

"There's nothing more I can give."

I answered his straight line sensibly. "You can give a little compensation for the mental anguish she suffered on account of what you did."

"Are you trying to blackmail me?"

"Anguish is a very real thing, Radfield. It works on a woman's general health. Her blood pressure goes skyrocketing up and her heart pumps blood so fast it might be damaged."

"I'll talk to the maid about it."

"No, you'll talk to me, Radfield. If we settle quickly, five hundred bucks will cover it."

24

"N-nonsense!"

"On the other hand, if I don't suddenly get sore and grab the money or a check out of your wallet right now, we can let a court decide. Miss Darling will tell the judge her side of the story and he's sure to fix damages pretty heavily."

"Now look here —"

"You're barrel-rolling a wrecked plane, Radfield. In this setup, five hundred isn't a lot of money to ask for. You know that much at least."

"Five hundred doesn't grow around like avocados," he muttered. "Well, I don't want to give the woman a hard time. I'll make out a check."

"Now there's just one more point," I said, pulling the check out of his hands as soon as he had written it. "I want to see Miss Wylie."

"Is that so? Well, she doesn't want to see anybody. She needs a lot of rest and she's getting it."

"I'll look in on her and see that for myself."

"Don't try it, Savage. I can't handle you personally, but I can get some of the special guards over here and they'll kick you out."

"Now listen." I leaned forward angrily. "If I don't see her in this hospital I'll see her after she gets out. There's just a chance she may be mad that you didn't let me talk to her before. I'm generally pretty persuasive with women."

Radfield looked resignedly at my six-two figure, his sad gaze resting on those broad shoulders of mine. There was no visible reason why even a so-called cold cookie like Lore Wylie might not suddenly take a shine to me or listen to my advising her to junk her current business manager.

"Look here, I don't even know who you are," he bleated. "You come in here with some story about a maid and now you want to see Miss Wylie. For all I know you could be a reporter and you'll write news bulletins that'll crucify her."

I stood up confidently, all set to walk over to Lore Wylie's room. Ignoring Radfield's quavery hesitation I said, "I work in the industry myself, and I make some of my living as a private detective. It's not an easy part-time buck, friend, but I get it because I'm dependable and I can be trusted with dirty linen. I've been told more than one man's share of stories in confidence, and I've kept all of them under my hat."

"Well, I suppose . . ."

"You can settle it easy enough," I said. "Miss Wylie works for Globe Studios, doesn't she? The top man there is Jules Schlosser, the Executive Vice President in charge of production. That means he's the one who kisses the bankers to get a picture financed. Call him long distance and ask him if he'd recommend Mark Savage to work for Miss Wylie. Do that, and you won't get conniptions while I'm talking to the girl."

Radfield scratched his jaw thoughtfully at a chance to let somebody else make a decision. Like any other buck-passer and student of delaying tactics, he had been dead for a long time but nobody had come along and told him to lie down, yet.

"All right, I'll do it," Radfield said firmly, getting up. "But I have to talk it over with Miss Wylie, too, before I decide whether or not she'll

26

see you."

"While you two are making up your minds, I'll be in conference with her."

"No. If I tell Miss Wylie not to talk to you till I've advised her, not to say a single word till I know more than I do now, Miss Wylie will positively listen to me."

I shrugged as if it didn't annoy me. "If you're going to do that, at least make the call from Miss Wylie's room so she can hear what Schlosser says."

"Yes, *of course* I'll do that. What do you take me for, anyhow?"

He bustled out of there. His steps hurried down the hall and then he called out urgently to an elevator operator to wait for him.

I waited restlessly. The sun's rays grew weaker. Dust tracks came into this austere room very gingerly and settled down on couches and ashtrays. I counted five fingers on each hand and wiggled five toes on each foot.

Radfield was hurrying when he got back, of course. He rushed in, nodded a greeting, and then gave me a weak smile that was curled around the edges by silent embarrassment. His eyes avoided my face.

"Mr. Schlosser is pretty well acquainted with you, from what I understand," he said finally. "Tole me you did a big job for him personally a couple of years back. I didn't catch all the details but he says you were very good. He says that if anybody can help Lore Wylie, you're the one."

"At least I didn't waste all my time waiting here."

"Mr. Schlosser is in favor of hiring you, so I

27

guess that settles it."

I was standing up before he finished. "What's Miss Wylie's room number?"

"*I'll* take you up to see Miss Wylie. I'm largely responsible for your seeing her, and I can introduce you and make sure you don't turn out to be a nuisance."

I burst out laughing.

## FOUR

The sickroom didn't have a trace of surgical white anywhere in its decor. The drapes were chocolate colored, the storage chest was a deep mahogany, and there was a green-and-black braided rug underfoot.

Lore Wylie flinched when I walked in with Radfield, and pulled the covers up to her shoulders. I gave a smile at even this distant contact with beauty. All natural redheads are very white-skinned, that's probably a union rule. Lore Wylie's skin might have just been exposed to daylight for the first time in her life. Without a trace of lipstick or powder, she looked like an attractive ghost. But the whiteness of her face was framed on three sides by deep red hair, and that combination made her beautiful.

"This is the first time a completely strange man has ever seen me in bed." That soft slurry voice brought back memories of half a dozen movies. "It makes me feel a little wicked and I've never liked that feeling."

"If you're all right otherwise, we can talk about what's bothering you. I had a long wait before I could get up here."

"There's nothing to say."

"You're in this place because you simply slashed your wrists. The sooner you tell me what made you do it, the sooner I can start to help you."

She chuckled without humor and suddenly met my frankness head-on.

"Quite a few things would have to be done, Mr. Savage. My career would have to be saved, not to mention my self-respect and maybe even my sanity. Could you do all those things, Mr. Savage?"

"As soon as I've got more details, I'll get started."

She became cautious the minute she saw me smile confidently. "And you expect me to talk honestly about myself to a stranger?"

"People have come to me in the past when things have been rough for them. Whatever I'm told means nothing to me, except as part of a job. I'm reliable, you know, and I get work from Hollywood people whenever I've got time to handle it."

"That sounds very noble!" Her lips thinned warily. "But how do I know you won't turn around and tell my story to all the newspapers?"

"Didn't Jules Schlosser give you some idea how reliable I am? Didn't he let you have a hint about what kind of a job I did for him once?"

"Well, he said you could put the squeeze on him for life if you had wanted to." She nibbled thoughtfully at her lower lip, which turned cherry red when she finally let it go from between her even white teeth. "He says you're good, Schlosser does, and he himself is a smart customer if ever I saw one."

"There you are, Lore! So I guess we can finally get started now."

"Mr. Savage, I wish you wouldn't — wait a minute! Are you the man named Savage who was hurt while shooting *King of the Rancho?*"

I shrugged at this additional delay. "Uh-huh.

That was a long time ago."

"How did it happen? I've always been curious about it. That is, if you feel like telling me."

"It won't take too long. I was supposed to do a simple 'drag' off a horse with my foot catching in a stirrup so that I bounced along for about twenty feet. An afternoon's easy work. But the damned horse suddenly changed direction on me because I made my drop a fraction of a second too soon and I cracked an ankle on account of it."

"I had my first love scene in that picture and it took three days to shoot because I was so uncomfortable," she murmured. "I can remember more details about that movie than about some of the ones I've made recently."

I wasn't surprised to hear Harold Radfield almost trip on the rug. He righted himself with difficulty and bent down to smooth the cuffs of his pants. He had to do it twice before the job was completed.

Lore looked up. "Why don't you step out and take care of some other things, Harry? I'll keep one hand on the bell just in case I need it all of a sudden."

"I'm not sure what has to be done."

"For one thing, you can tell those TV people that I won't act the part of a dance-hall girl on that western program." She shuddered. "Absolutely not."

"All right, but I'd like to be sure that — uh, Mr. Savage, knows about the money arrangement."

"I was going to tell him, Harry, that Jules Schlosser agreed over the phone that the studio would pay the bill, and Mr. Savage's services won't cost me anything."

"As long as it's straightened out, that's all I wanted to know. Well, take care of yourself, Lore, and do what the nurses tell you." He got to his feet, dropped the monocle into a breast pocket, and didn't glance back at me till he reached the door. "Nice to have — uh," he said lamely, and walked out.

The shadow of a smile twisted Lore's full lips as she looked after him. "He's a crazy one even for my town. He has to dress like a maniac, work in chaos, and live on the thin edge of bankruptcy. But he handles other people's money with the accent on gilt-edged safety investments. That's why he's trusted in spite of everything."

"Forget Radfield now and tell me about yourself, Lore. What's gone wrong? Tell me the truth."

She stared down at the yellow-and-orange Danish blanket under which her hands had been hidden all this time. Her face whitened a little further, which I wouldn't have thought was possible with her. She looked like a bleached cloud.

"Well, you know, it's hard for an actress to get near the top of a murderous business like mine without being willing to do almost anything if there's a payoff. An aspiring actress has to be ready to cut throats or slip into bed with a fat old producer if a good part will come her way for doing it."

"So?"

"Well, the point is that I didn't do any of those things. My business life may not be much better

32

than most people's, but my love life has been clean. Spotless, in fact, that way. If you can say that a woman of 25 in my business is morally clean, I'm that woman and proud of it."

"Okay, Lore, what's the catch?"

"There's a photograph of — well, it looks just like me together with a man and — and —"

"Take it easy, Lore, from the beginning. When did you find out about this?"

"Yesterday I received a clasp envelope in the mail. It had my name and address typewritten on it, but no return address. I opened it and saw a glossy six-by-nine picture of — I'd have almost sworn it was me and a man naked together."

"Who was the man?"

"I don't know him. I never saw him in my life. He was as strange to me as you were when you walked in here. I haven't got the slightest idea who he was." She shivered. "And what was being done in that picture was dreadful. Unspeakably vile."

"Maybe the picture had been retouched. Suppose your face was put on another body, somehow. It can be done that way, you know."

"No, it wasn't an imposition of any kind, Mr. Savage. Not this time. The girl in that photograph is somebody who looks just like me, almost a twin sister. Nobody would believe it wasn't me, but I never did anything like that. I never could!"

I stroked my jaw, a gesture which is supposed to make me look thoughtful. "Were you asked for money?"

"There wasn't anything else in the envelope but that photograph. I haven't been asked or told or shown anything more by whoever sent it to me.

**33**

That was all."

"Go ahead."

"I went to ask Harry Radfield's advice about it that afternoon. I didn't want to spring the story on him right away. The shock would be almost overpowering. He knew what a good reputation I have. I started quietly by asking if he'd ever heard anything about me that even smelled of a scandal."

"And he'd heard something?"

"Well, he hemmed and hawed for a while, and made business-agent noises. I started to realize that *he* was preparing *me* for something. He finally said that he'd been told that there's a silent 'stag' movie of me doing things like — like that girl does in the photograph."

"How did he know about the stag movie? Had he seen it?"

"Not personally, he said, but I can't be sure he hasn't. Or that thousands of people haven't seen it and that they don't snigger and sneer every time they see a real movie of mine. You know, that hateful terrible way that most men have."

"*I* don't have, Lore, and I like women. I've given them a lot of pleasure and they've given me a lot. Why shouldn't I like them?"

"I would think that most men who are so successful with women wouldn't care much for them. It'd seem to me that those men are contemptuous of women because it's easy to get them and the women fall for the same approach."

"Is that what you think?" I stared. "Whoever's been telling you about sex doesn't know much or care for what she thinks she does know."

"Well, I — my mother always says that she's

34

been happily married for thirty years." Lore sighed. "Whenever I feel I like a man I can imagine my mother telling me not to do anything important with him till after I'm married to him. Time after time she used to tell me that when I was smaller. My father would look a little embarrassed and give out hints that he agreed with her."

"You should have belted both of them," I said.

"Oh, this is hopeless, all of it," Lore suddenly called out, her body shaking under the covers. "I don't know who sent that vile picture to me or why. There isn't anything I can say or do that'll prove what a lie it is. Everybody knows that actresses have doubles, look-alikes; but nobody would believe that some woman who resembles me very closely must have . . ."

"We can worry about that when we have to," I started to say quickly.

But she interrupted, giving me an accusing look as if she'd suddenly thought of something bad about me. "I'll bet that *you* don't believe I never did anything like that. You're not sure. I'll bet you aren't sure."

"What I think doesn't cut any ice," I said quietly. "It won't make my job easier or harder. Let's pull ourselves together and get back to the things that happened, Lore. You decided to kill yourself — and then what did you do?"

"Made my preparations, of course. I wrote a letter saying that I couldn't keep on living. Then I got a knife from the kitchen and went to the bathroom to do the job. At the last minute I remembered that photograph, so I tore it up and burned the pieces."

"Oh, I see. At least now I know what happened to it. That alone was giving a few people some grief, you know, Lore."

"Yes. Harry told me when I came to that he took it for granted the picture was some place in my hotel suite. He knew I had it, but it wasn't in sight. Anyhow, he accused the chambermaid of having stolen it and gave her a terrible time, the poor woman. I'll have to send her an extra present to make up for it."

"All right, Lore. Just one other question and it's something I always ask. It doesn't mean I've got eyes in the back of my head or that I'm accusing you of anything. All I want to know is whether you're hiding any facts from me. Anything at all that might help."

"No."

"It wouldn't pay for you if you tried. That's like hiding symptoms from a doctor or papers from a lawyer or figures from an accountant. I can't do a good job if I haven't got all of it."

"There's nothing more, I give you my word." She paused. "Tell *me* something, now. Can you do this thing in such a way that my name won't come into it?"

"I'll try the best I can."

"If anything goes wrong and my parents find out or anybody else even suspects what happened, Mr. Savage, I won't be able to take it. I'm not going to spend the rest of my life in hiding, with men staring at me in that sniggering, disgusting way of theirs."

"If the story does come out everybody will know that you were victimized." I was on my way to the door, anxious to start working.

"People will say, 'There's no smoke without fire,' and that sort of thing. There'll always be some who think I really posed for pictures like that. I couldn't stand it, I simply couldn't stand it!"

"You can't help it unless you slash your wrists again. Better yet, try poison next time. It's more likely to get the trick accomplished."

She didn't protest at my unfeeling remark, which was the opposite of what I'd have expected from a woman who was playing a scene. Instead she nodded slowly.

"I'll work steady on it and do the best I can," I said quietly. "If it's possible I'll try to report every day. Don't do anything till you hear a few reports."

"I don't suppose you're any better than most men, but I ought to thank you for what you'll be trying to do."

"It's not a public service," I said gruffly, opening the door. "I'm getting paid for it."

"Yes, of course." A softer color came into her cheeks. She tried to smile, but her wavering lips snapped back to the familiar grim line. "Consider yourself thanked very sincerely."

"Consider yourself told that you're welcome."

I wasn't feeling chipper on my way to the elevator. Not that it grieved me too much knowing that a girl of her coldness to men or prudishness, whichever it was, could ironically get into a jam like this; I wasn't going to let myself get spooked on account of it, though. There was something a hell of a lot more important for me to worry about.

Remembering that white, determined face and the thrust-out chin, I warned myself not to make any bloopers about Lore Wylie. If there was so much as a hint of scandal about her, Lore Wylie would try killing herself again. It was plain that she had decided to keep clear of any morals trouble even if it meant cashing in her chips such a short time after having bought into the game. A circus acrobat I trained with once said to me at a bull session that a promiscuous woman wins male friends but no respect, a selective woman wins male friends but no respect from the ones who are favored, and the genuinely moral Lore Wylie type wins everybody's respect but damn few friends, male or female. Lore Wylie needed on male friend at least and for as long as this trouble lasted she'd have him for sure.

But it meant that I was working under more pressure than usual to get definite results. A woman's life was part of the stakes in this assignment.

The elevator hadn't come after two full minutes of waiting, so I swore at the machine, as well as its operators, and practically hurled myself down the stairs.

There was one pleasant chore to tackle. I couldn't help whistling under my breath as I put the check for Lynne Darling into an envelope addressed to her at the Beckwin. After I told her on the phone that the unexpected check to soothe her wounded feelings would be in the next day's mail, she started praising me to the skies. The sameness of her remarks, complimentary though they were, was enough to set my teeth on edge and I glared at the slow-moving minute hand of the watch I wore.

Harold Radfield was much too busy to see me today, he insisted when I phoned him at the Dortmund Hotel over on Fifty-third and Fifth. After he recited the two or three matters he needed to handle, I let him know I'd meet him in the lobby of his hotel for a few minutes at least.

He was almost effusive the third time I talked to him, shaking my hand warmly before we sat down on oversized chairs. "Lore just told me on the phone that you two got along very well, and I'm almost ashamed to say I made her repeat it three times."

I brushed that aside. "How did you come to hear about a 'hot' movie Lore was supposed to have appeared in?"

"Oh, that. Well, I have a friend — an acquaintance, actually. He's a liar and I've often been victimized by his simple-minded practical jokes. So when he told me about this movie I figured it was another joke of his until Lore told me about having received a photograph in the mail."

"Has this friend of yours seen the movie?"

"I wouldn't be surprised. He runs showings of that kind of thing in his apartment once every two weeks."

"When's the next show?"

"Very soon, but I'm not sure I remember when."

"Tonight, maybe?"

"I'm not absolutely sure, but I think so," Radfield admitted when I pressed him further.

"Were you invited?" I asked bluntly.

"Well, there was a suggestion . . ."

"And you said no," I finished for him. "Call this guy up and tell him you're sending an acquaintance along, instead."

"*You* want to go? Well, I'm not sure — that is, I can imagine the sort of thing you'll tell the fellow."

"Do you want to come along as peacemaker?" I grinned.

"It isn't funny." A look of pain returned to the suntanned face and he nearly crashed a fist into that precious monocle of his. "I think somebody ought to go along and make sure that — well, see how you handle yourself on a job."

"Maybe you'll learn something," I agreed. "What time does the show start?"

"Either at eight or half-past. I'm not sure which."

"I'll pick you up in this lobby at eight o'clock on the head."

"I'm not sure if I can make that. I've got some other arrangements and I have to take care of them, too."

"If you don't make it I'll go up to your room and break the door in, just to prove my point."

Radfield blanched, then asked mildly, "Are you — uh, joking?"

"A little, but not too much."

Radfield relaxed, chuckled, and said that he knew I'd do a good job. He insisted on shaking my hand to seal the new friendship.

# FIVE

It was a bachelor apartment at First Avenue in the Sixties tht Harold Radfield led me into that night. There were rush chairs in the living room off the foyer, pine panelling wallpaper, and a stuffed moosehead against one wall flanked by two racks of sporting rifles.

A tall bronzed man with thick, black eyebrows and a hawk nose was handling a Mossberg 620K single-shot chuckster by its inletted Circassian walnut stock when I walked into the room. He turned around, remembered the gun, put it back meticulously in its place on several old-fashioned square nails in one of the mahogany racks and turned with a hard, brown hand stretched out to me.

"Glad to see you, though I wasn't expecting you or Rad," he said heartily in a deep booming baritone that rolled around us like summer thunder. "I'm Charlie Osterman."

"Mark Savage."

Osterman gave me a firm handshake. He had been chewing tobacco a little while ago, and brown stains descended in small jagged rows from the corners of his mouth. He was wearing a sportshirt unbuttoned to show the wiry black hair on his sun-darkened chest.

Osterman stepped away from me and glanced behind him at the weapons. "Do you know anything about guns, Savage? By Christ, I hope so. For your own sake. A man's no goddamn good if he can't fire a gun, if he don't know how to kill a moose with a .338 Magnum, for instance. Best moose gun in the world. I don't care who the hell a man is, he's no goddamn good if he can't do that."

"I fired a gun once," I said softly.

"Look at those beauties on the other rack! Genuine percussion muzzle-loaders, all of 'em. And they're in shooting condition, hell, yes. They're rifled, with round barrels and brass fittings. I don't have to tell anybody I keep 'em polished like new."

"All I wanted to know about is the stag movies you show here sometimes."

"Like the ones we're going to show tonight, you mean?" Osterman rolled down a home movie screen that looked like an off-color window shade. "Me and some other people get together once every two weeks and look at hot pictures. We get a boot out of doing it and anybody who don't like that can take it and shove it! There are too goddamn many mental and spiritual old maids in this country, I tell you."

"Who do you get the stag movies from?"

"Some joker bastard who charges too goddamn much, that's who." Osterman grunted. "He must be supplying at least a hundred 'art study' groups in and around the city, not to mention extra calls from stag dinners and smokers. Oh, he's doing all right, believe me . . . by the way, you can drop your dough on the little table against that wall."

42

"Dough?"

"Ten green men apiece. Most of them go to the guy I rent the movies from. Anything that comes into my pockets isn't enough to ram up a cockroach's left nostril. If I was part of the business for real, I wouldn't be using no cheap crap like this stuff is. A 16 millimeter silent that runs to a couple hundred feet is just about the cheapest there is."

"Who's the guy you rent these pictures from?"

"I don't want to talk about that bum because it gets me too mad thinking how much loot he makes out of an operation like this one. Hell with him!"

I'd have tried to get some answers if I had to stuff a pneumatic bullet up Charlie Osterman's nostrils and hit him with the barrel of his Winchester .22 match rifle. But a man walked in furtively just then and so did another and a third. None of them smiled. One guy talked briefly. The seven newcomers who finally came inside were men of all ages — and in all stages. A couple of oldsters. A few in their 20's. A man in his 40's who sat licking his lips and blowing invisible dust off a spotless dark suit. A man in his 30's whose dark-complected face must have been splotched at birth.

One woman came in a little later. She was tall and thin, with too much make-up, ample breasts and firmly-shaped thighs. She sat down next to a boy in his 20's, and the boy turned to her with a diffident smile.

Osterman tested the projector with blunt stubby fingers, then suddenly took a pace backwards as I watched him and cut the lights. Radfield cleared his throat half a dozen times.

The sixteen millimeter movie began with a scrawled clumsy-looking title card. The movie was called, A Schoolgirl Learns Her Lesson. The cheap picture had either been lighted badly or the film had been exposed too soon. A nude woman and two fully clothed men appeared in the first few frames, the men circling the woman. Suddenly the woman turned to one of them and started fumbling with the buttons of his pants.

Above the humming projector I could hear the hard breathing from the audience. The backwash of light from the screen showed me one of the college age kids sitting as if he'd been hypnotized, jaw hanging down and eyes wide open. The woman sitting next to him was moistening her lips furiously with her gleaming tongue. Radfield stared at the screen with unwilling and revolted fascination.

The movie came to a halt. Shamefaced silence was broken by Osterman whistling cheerfully under his breath as he set up two more films that could be shown without pause from the same reel.

"You want to know something?" Osterman suddenly asked the uneasy audience. "You're all hungry to see a hot movie like this, but when it's over you hate yourselves. You haven't got the courage of your desires, if that makes any sense. In other words, you're a crew of lard-ass bastards."

Nobody said a word to contradict that.

"And goddamn it, these movies show a perfectly normal taste that every guy's got. It's showing what plenty of men dream about. Anybody who says that's not true is talking through his left eyeball. What the hell! A guy's got red blood in his veins, not warm water."

I noticed Radfield polishing his monocle with fanatic attention as the next batch of movies started.

On the screen a breasty blonde was taking a man's shirt off and then his underwear. The man lay inert on a bed, his eyes closed and his face rigid; but it was easy to see in the body angle that he wasn't dead. I turned away and gestured to Charlie Osterman. He shook his head once and stared at the screen, but I got his attention again. He growled and crooked a forefinger at me. I followed him gingerly to the small kitchen with a glass door, which he closed. He then stood looking out at what appeared on the movie screen.

"There's something I want to know," I started.

"Well, maybe I'll tell you and maybe I won't."

"Did you ever hear about a stag movie with a famous actress in it?"

"Let me tell you," He started bragging, then cut it. He glanced away from the distant screen and ran a hard hand thoughtfully along the line of his bronzed, belligerent jaw and narrowed his eyes in my direction, as if I was a pound of meat on a butcher's scale. "You're a friend of Rad's, you claim. Are you out to make trouble on account of a little talking I did when I was with Rad once? I must have been higher than a kite to tell him some of the things I told him that time."

"You asked the question; you answer it."

"I got more important things to do than stand around answering questions from snotnose friends of Rad's. I'll give you a little piece of advice for free, though: get the hell out of here before I plant a shoe up your tail."

"I want to know who you rent those pictures from."

"Screw you!"

"Who do you rent them from, Osterman? Tell me that and I'll be on my way out of here."

"You're on the way out now, buster. Right this minute."

He began moving forward slowly and shrewdly with his big body in a hard-to-hit crouch, his fingers wide apart to give striking speed. The arrogant self-confidence belonged to a man who must have been on the winning end of any number of barroom brawls.

"Let's see how good you do," he said with ferocious amiability, "when you're up against a real man."

I smiled contemptuously. He was trying to scare me gutless by coming at me slowly. Worrying the other guy is a barroom brawler's big stock-in-trade whether he takes his time or tries a fast roaring rush. He's not likely to have much else on the ball when you get down to it, so he wants to make you run like hell.

Ten feet away Osterman rushed me. I had already come forward to meet him. With my left hand I grabbed his right sleeve and pivoted, balancing myself on one foot. I grabbed for his right leg with my other hand. Then I bent over. Osterman's big body, heaviest at the stomach, was rolled along my back. He plopped down on the floor, red-faced with anger.

"Bastard!"

He rolled over and stood up quickly, darting one hand into a pocket as part of the change in tactics. It flashed up with a compact hunting knife, the stubby, shiny blade extended at me. This time he rushed me almost before I could see him at it.

I chopped the flat of one palm against the side of his neck. Osterman gaped at me as if I'd broken a rule he had made. Shock alone brought white streaks under his tan and froze him briefly. He dropped with one solid motion, like a tree. A sudden startled gasp was pushed through Osterman's lips as he hit the floor. Redness appeared on his chest and dribbled down. The tip of the knife, close to him, was stained dard. His face showed nothing more than irritation at the sight of part of his masculine strength dribbling out of him.

"A goddamn scratch!" he said with determined indifference. "I can still take you on, right now."

"You'll have to, if I don't find out what I want to know."

"Okay. How come you're waiting till I get up?"

"If I have to hit you again, it'll hurt more when you're standing."

"You're full of it, buddy."

"If you don't tell me who rents you those movies, you'll find out for yourself if I'm full of it."

"I'm getting up right now, and I'll finish you this time."

He lurched to one side and my eyes, following him, were distracted by the mirror at my left. It showed what was on the screen. The woman had stripped the inert man till he was as naked as a turkey, and she was now kissing his chest. Then her tongue spaded his navel. There was a sudden murmur outside and I saw two black figures leap against the screen light and then fall below it together. Rhythmic applause swept the audience. The onlookers' obvious pleasure at such artificial stimulation made me feel queasy.

"Now I'll really take care of . . . ."

I looked at Osterman again; he had stopped talking very quickly. As I turned to him, sudden surprise forced his thick lips open and betrayed him into glancing at my right.

I turned to see a hard, angry, strange face made more taut by a vicious, wolfish smile. Even as I brought up a hand against the newcomer, there was a motion above the corner of my eye. Something came down hard against one side of my head, lowering me into a black-tinged grayness, a near-unconscious state. My knees buckled and I dropped.

Pain stretched from the top of my head downward. There wasn't a skin graft on me that didn't tingle; even the caps of my teeth seemed to be knifing the gums.

It took me a few minutes to realize that two sets of noises were going on not very far from me. One set was the dentist-drill hum of the projector and applause from the audience at what was going on either in a 16 millimeter stag movie or on the floor among them. Or both.

The other set of noises was made up of a low rumble like thunder alternating with higher-pitched and faster sound. Voices, in fact. Two men talking.

The lower-pitched one, Osterman's, was saying, "That goddamn scratch isn't hurting me!"

"If the bandage I just made don't hold you, see a sawbones," the other responded briskly. "At least you didn't get hurt where you might be no good to a broad."

"That'll never happen to me," Osterman put in very quickly. "I'd use my big toe with a broad, if I had to."

"And this creep you were mixing it up with, you don't know who he is?"

"Never saw the goddamn bum before in my whole life."

"Let me see what he's got on him."

The newcomer did it very cleverly, pulling my jacket down far enough so that I wasn't able to move my arms. But I wouldn't have had the strength to raise a finger if he'd asked me to. I hadn't opened my eyes yet.

"It says here in his wallet card that his name is Mark Savage," the newcomer said, after a pause, "and it gives an address in California. The ID card says he's a private eye. A goddamn snoop . . . When he comes out of it, Osterman, clobber him around till you're damn certain he won't be back again."

"It'll be a pleasure."

"Okay, Osterman. I'm scramming out of here. Behind schedule as it is. It's bad for business when one of the messengers louses up the schedule, you know."

"Wait till the last reel is over, for God's sake! That boss of yours is probably a zillionaire already."

"Wouldn't be a bit surprised. Okay, I'll wait a

few minutes. Where's the dough? The sooner I get that, the better I feel."

"It's on the hall table."

"I'll grab that first, and maybe," he chuckled, "I can have myself a little fun out there. The customers are sure getting their money's worth in extra activities — huh, Osterman?"

"Yes, and I have to be here, of all the crummy goddamn luck. Get one for me, will you, Ziggy?"

"Get your own broad. If I grab two I'll take care of 'em both."

I heard the heavy footsteps of the man called Ziggy going toward the direction of the door and managed to open my eyes long enough to get a first glimpse of him. He looked even bigger than he actually was from where I lay. He walked with a muscular swing to his steps and carried a black leather suitcase.

From a distance I heard Harold Radfield saying hoarsely, "I'm getting out of this place if I can only find the damned door!" and the rhythmic applause soared again at something else that was happening in that other room.

The projector stopped whirring finally. Men shuffled to the door at a funereal pace. Two women followed, one of them walking erratically on high heels as breath rasped out from her narrowed throat. The door closed softly, in time. A man hurried out of the bathroom, then pounded to the door and slammed it back of him. Ziggy, if my guess was any good.

Slowly, patiently, I opened my eyes and tried to get up. The first dizzy spell I'd had in years passed over me and faded away. Osterman was staring at me from his position halfway across the room. He touched a hand nervously against the right side of his chest, which looked big on account of the bandage Ziggy had put on him.

"Stay where the hell you are," he blustered. "I've got this and it's loaded."

He was holding a bright nickel-plated Smith & Wesson .38 Special aimed now at my belly button, now at my left ear.

"I'm not coming after you," I said tiredly, seeing that the safety was off. "I forgot to bring a pencil sharpener to kill you with."

"Son of a bitch! I'll shoot."

"Then you'll go to the chair and you know it, or you wouldn't have put the safety on." I shrugged. "You've got a piece of steel in your hand and nothing else."

"Don't get smart with me!"

I decided not to try and get any information out of him; it might be possible to reach Ziggy first and to let him lead me to his boss.

"One more thing, Osterman. I'm walking out of here as of now."

I turned slowly and managed to get out of that room, down the living room and out the foyer over to the door. Once I nearly fell because I was so anxious to find the messenger. Dizziness swept over me. It was the longest trip I had ever taken. One time on a stunt I crash-landed a Boeing 707 by myself and skidded it half a mile; but I couldn't have spent as much time on it as I spent walking the seventy-five feet or so out of Charlie Osterman's apartment.

I drew a deep breath when I reached the wide

dim-lit hallway. There wasn't much time to waste if I was going to get on that messenger's tracks and eventually find out who his boss was. I saved a little time by taking the stairs down.

## SIX

For once I was playing in luck. Those streaks
come along in both my businesses when you don't
expect them. In fact, you hardly know what's
happening at the time. It doesn't occur to you that
you've had a break till later on, when you come to
think it over. By then, it goes without saying,
you've lucked out all over again.

But I did have it good at the start. The cold
brisk February night air cleared my head right
away. Stunt men seem to recover from injuries
more quickly than most people do, which is a fact
I can't explain, but it's true just the same. I could
see every inch of First Avenue and Sixty-sixth by
the efficient fluorescent street lights. Ziggy was
walking to the sidewalk's edge, having been
delayed by the stopover upstairs for a little cheap
sex.

I put on a fresh burst of speed when I saw him
getting into a car. Ten feet away from it, though,
as I made a surprisingly shaky fist to persuade the
hood to talk, I saw a Yellow Cab approaching. The
driver stopped almost directly in front of me when
he made out my urgent signals.

"Follow the car at your right and a little in front of you."

"Follow it?"

"Yes, follow the damn thing. The one that looks like a custom job."

The driver turned his head to stare at the almost surgically white Chev that Ziggy was settling down in, a '56 model with its emblem and hood ornaments stripped along with every other horizontal bar on the front grille. The sight of the frenched headlights made him wince.

"Mister," he said to me, "I don't go around following no cars. I'm not aiming to get in trouble."

"Oh for God's — look here, twenty bucks says you don't really mind doing this job for me."

"Twenty bucks?"

"It's right here in my hand. If you do what I want, I'll give it to you; if you don't I'm liable to shove it down your throat."

"Is that twenty bucks over the tab?"

"Sure."

The hackie sighed. "I guess my code 'a ethics is pretty elastic at that, when you come right down to it."

My driver did his job for the next few minutes. I sat on the edge of the seat and swore at the traffic obstructions, the red lights and the daredevil pedestrians who crossed against the lights during the all-too-brief intervals that favored us.

Ziggy drove purposefully, like a rat who knows a shortcut through the maze. He piloted that steel snowflake down First to Fifty-seventh and upwards to Eighth, picking his way carefully and shrewdly past the other cars on the streets and turning down Eighth. A parking space on the northeast corner of Twenty-seventh caught his eye and he eased the car deftly into it.

The hackie made a half-turn in my direction.

"Want to wait for him?"

"Damned if I wait around for the likes of him," I said.

"I'd have to cruise a little because there's no more parking spaces, but we'd pick him up real fast as soon as he started going in that kooked-up wheelbarrow he drives."

"No cruising, no waiting," I said roughly. "The hell with that crap."

A car passed close enough to scrape the soles off my shoes as I left that cab, but I didn't step back. As soon as I had overpaid for the ride, I bucked the red light and ran to the sidewalk.

My eyes were fixed on Ziggy and that black leather briefcase. He passed a movie marquee advertising Spanish language pix, and some shabby stores, and boys with long sideburns talking to girls who had grown up too fast. One of the big-breasted girls called out something admiring as I passed, but I walked without turning my head in acknowledgment. My fingers made fists and then unmade them as I tried to keep myself from running up to Ziggy and choking the truth out of him.

He dived into a shabby-looking brownstone building with too many windows and floors to be a public bathroom. The hand-painted sign over the entrance said that the place was a hotel and the dirt-caked sign directly under it said that transients were accommodated. The owners probably did a roaring business with transient couples who wanted a room for half an hour only, and didn't care if the place could never be mistaken for the Waldorf Astoria as long as it had a double bed in it somewhere.

There was no sign of Ziggy in the wide, old-fashioned lobby. The high-backed chairs and splotchy sofas had gone out of style in the eighteen nineties, but the harsh direct lighting had stayed around for a couple of years more. A raddled looking woman in her sixties stood watching me alertly from her position back of a wooden counter at the far side of this museum. Her dark brown eyes could probably x-ray a man's wallet at forty paces and measure the lint in a woman's pocketbook across the street. She wouldn't have trusted ten fingers scratching her back.

Now she looked me up and down. "What's yours, mister?"

"The man who just came in here," I said authoritatively, quietly. "I want to know which room he went to."

She growled, "If you've got a potsy, show it."

"I've got nothing but money. Twenty bucks."

"I'll take fifty."

"You'll get ten now and ten on my way out, if you don't tip off the people that I'm coming. That's my last offer."

"Mister, you look a lot too anxious. If that's your last offer, you can kiss me good-bye. I'll show you where."

"The odds are that I'll kick you good-bye,

instead." I drew a twenty and a five out of my wallet. "Half now and half later."

The money disappeared without a move being made that I could see. There was a slight flick around the v of her thin polka dot dress and a papery bump appeared between her wafer-thin breasts. That was all.

"Room twenty-six, mister. On the second floor, six doors from your left as you get off the stairs."

She pointed a beefy thumb towards the row of steps the color of weak tea at the right of her counter. I scooted that way and ignored the creak when my soles punished step number one, and the dust on the bannister that did a little eccentric dance when it was dislodged. My brain was fixed firmly on the idea of getting to room twenty-six on the second floor, six doors from my left as I go off the stairs.

Ziggy was just closing the door of room twenty-six when I reached the floor. He was an ugly hatchet-faced guy, as I saw now, and the face was temporarily disfigured by a small relieved smile. His briefcase was almost flat now, and set at a jaunty angle.

He turned his back without seeing me and started walking down the narrow dusty hall. As I followed, his footsteps suddenly pounded down a staircase at the far end of the hall. My eyes reluctantly left the direction in which he'd disappeared and turned to the door of room twenty-six. I nodded firmly to myself. Without hesitating any longer, I turned the knob and pushed the door open.

The smells of stale perfume and liquor assaulted

my nostrils before I found the light switch and pressed it. Light made the smells stronger somehow by giving evidence to the eyes. A pair of empty whiskey bottles lay on the thinly carpeted floor and tendrils of long black woman's hair were sprawled across them and gleaming like part of a spider's web. Five cans of film had been stacked on the floor at the other side of the whiskey bottles.

The wide double bed held a parody newspaper with the headline: JERRY HITS NEW YORK; MEN ORDERED TO LOCK UP THEIR DAUGHTERS. There was a plastic ahstray in the shape of a reclining nude, an empty carton of L&M's and dozens of burnt matches. A baby-sized doll dressed as a Southern belle of Civil War times had been put down beside a box of silly putty.

The only tenant of this room was sleeping heavily across the bed with a pillow at his feet and two of them beneath his head. He wore one blue stocking as well as crumpled, dark blue underpants and a soiled undershirt. He was a short fellow without a hair on him from the neck up, and his head was shaped like a football. He looked like nothing I'd ever seen outside a zoo.

I slammed the door. He didn't move. I called out. Nothing. Again. Not even a word from him. I bent over and cursed him loudly and vilely enough to have made Studs Lonigan blush. He might have been a statue for all it meant to him.

There was a water pitcher with a cracked handle on the night table. I flung its contents into his face. He howled in a high voice, sputtered, opened his eyes and then glared at me.

"Yer no better 'n a ponce, that's what," he

grumbled finally, reaching out for a towel next to the uniform of a British seaman on the floor. "Bloody ruddy ponce!"

"I don't know what you're talking about," I said brusquely, and decided on taking a chance. He was too groggy to realize what might be going on. This was the morning after a big night for him. He couldn't have been awake for hours so the odds were good that he was not very likely to spot a certain lie when he heard it. I kicked at the cans of film. "Brought you a present, limey."

"You did, hey?" He squinted up at me. "Where's Ziggy? What become o' him?"

"Ziggy's mother sent a note asking to have him excused."

"Very funny." He swiped at his face with the towel, but rubbed both lips with the back of a hand. Maybe that was his notion of hygiene. "Well, all right, so you did it. Don't 'ave to be such a bleeding pig about it."

"I wanted you to know it was there, limey. Otherwise, you might have forgot to look around when you woke up."

"Listen 'ere! Ziggy 'as left the stuff off with me a million times. It always works out as easy as kiss-me-'and. There's never no trouble. Because why? Because Ziggy does 'is job and I do mine, and we don't do no more."

"Is that right?"

"It sure is. Ziggy leaves the cans and I re-roll the film and bring it back 'ome. All I tell the people at customs is that I'm carrying film what 'asn't been exposed yet. Well, they're not going to go prying into that and spoil the film for me. I pay a small duty and that's all. Works like a charm, it does. And those crummy movies get a big play up and down the bleeding empire, what's left of it."

I nodded as if this was stale old news to me. I might have known that a movie wouldn't ever be exhausted. Probably it travelled up and down Europe as well as into Asia. This was like Marshall Plan aid with kicks in it.

"Okay, limey," I said with a cheerful smile that would have been perfectly genuine on a three dollar bill. "I'll give Ziggy your regards and have him come down personally next time."

"Yerss! Ziggy's a lad what has got feelings and 'uman decency." He drew both hands up to his head and rocked back and forth. "Me 'ead's bustin', and all you can do is stand there and make small talk."

He'd have struck me as a nice guy ordinarily, a bald little Britisher who probably had hundreds of friends and got a big boot out of drifting around or he wouldn't have been in the Royal Navy. A harmless, happy-go-lucky seaman — but his sideline wasn't good clean fun at all. It was soul-destroying and damnable, instead. I had all I could do to keep from beating hell out of him in spite of his hangover.

"I'm getting out of here," I said evenly. "Anybody else I can give your regards to?"

"Uh-uh. All a bunch 'a perishin' bleeders is what they are. It stands to reason. Anybody in a business like yours would 'ave to be a perishin' bleeder."

"Even the boss?"

"Stands to reason, though I never met him. I

60

don't even know his name, and I only met Goodell once at a party, and got talking to him. But it was pure accident."

"Anybody else you've met besides Goodell?" I asked, trying to sound casual.

"Not a ruddy one."

I nodded reluctantly. A man on his low level in the outfit didn't have to tell much before his brains would be picked clean. Talking to him amounted to nothing more than to take a stained step up a filthy ladder.

He suddenly drew a long black hair from the bed, leaned forward, and said confidentially, "Y'know, I don't mind going to bed with prosties. In one way it's like a business deal. Tit for tat, as the sayin' goes. And I got more respect for a girl like that than for one 'a those sweet-faced bitches who works in an office and figures on marrying a nice young bloke with a future and being a parasite for the rest of her life." He winced. "But lor' lumme, why do I always feel so damned rotten afterwards? . . . I wish you'd leave me alone, mate. I might not 'ave mentioned it before, but I've got a 'eadache."

The beady-eyed landlady or night clerk, whichever she was, waited for me at the foot of the stairs. Her eyes x-rayed the wallet in my pocket, and one of those greasy palms was stretched out towards me.

"You owe twenty-five dollars," she said precisely.

I handed over the money, but didn't wait around to see it disappear magically like the other bills had done. A gilt-framed mirror showed the woman walking cautiously around the desk just as I got out of there.

## SEVEN

At half-past nine next morning, I stepped out of
a cab with Rex in front of the Dutch County
Hospital. It was the second warm February day in
a row, and the sudden sky-rocketing temperature
was making New Yorkers dress comfortably for a
change and talk about summer vacations as if
they'd be coming up very soon now.

My collie stood by in a ladylike fashion while I
paid the fare and walked, over to open the main
entrance door for her. She swished her tail
exultantly on walking into the strange lobby and
seeing people turn toward her. Rex is nothing if
not a lady.

The receptionist was the same elderly
prune-faced woman who'd hated the idea of letting
me into the visitor's room yesterday afternoon.
"You say you spoke to Miss Wylie's doctor and he
agreed to permit a dog to visit here? A dog? I've
never heard of anything like thi — Please don't take
that attitude with me. You're the most impatient
man I ever met in my life. Just a moment and I'll
phone upstairs . . . Very well. I can't understand it,
but the nurse agrees with what you say. And our
standards at Dutch County always used to be so
*high.*"

Rex sniffed at a young intern's hand during the elevator ride, steadily ignoring the attendant and patient who tried to make friends with her. I guess that every female goes for a doctor.

As soon as Lore Wylie saw us coming she did the first prudish thing I'd have expected, drawing up the blanket till it covered her to the chain and raising that blanket very slightly so I was unable to see her figure underneath it. I couldn't remember a colder reception since the time I crashed a Fairchild P-26 into the freezing waters of Lake Michigan as part of a war picture.

"I can't get used to any man seeing me like this," she admitted, her set face even whiter than usual. "I keep hearing my mother say that a man only wants one thing, no matter what he claims he's after."

"Your mother must have had a wonderful love life," I said brusquely, getting that out of the way before I could make report number one.

But she asked, "Why did you bring a dog, Mr. Savage? Did you have some sort of crackpot idea that I'll like you better if I know that you've got a dog?"

"That's part of it," I conceded with more patience than I'd known was in me. "The other parts are simply that you might snap out of the blues a little and that my collie enjoys changes of scenery every once in a while and that I can't take care of her myself for every minute."

"I suppose you keep a dog because that way it's easier to get friendly with women," Lore said. "It makes you seem domestic, and once you've made that point with a woman it's probably easier to get

64

all you want from her."

"Rex and I help each other get action, if you really want to know." I brushed that aside sardonically. "And don't ask about the name because it'll only keep me from getting to business that much quicker."

"*Is* anything new on the case? Harry Radfield told me that he started out with you last night, but that he couldn't stand the pace and he got away as fast as he could."

"Which wasn't too fast, as far as I know," I told her. "About the case: things aren't as definite as I would like, but there's been some small progress and I might very well have definite information next time I see you. What I'm trying to get across is that you shouldn't give up, whatever you do."

"I hope you're right. God, I hope you can prove that a double for me made that filthy movie, or you destroy it or do both. I couldn't stand it for the public to think that I, of all people, could possibly have ever been in a stag movie."

"Well, I'm going to get busy on it again right now, Lore."

"Oh, wait! You're in such a hurry you forgot to take the dog."

"Rex is staying with you till I get back."

"But won't she think she's being — uh — given away to me?"

"She knows I wouldn't do that," I said shortly. "Slip her a pound and a half or so of chopped raw beef in a blue bowl and a cup of cooked vegetables for dinner if I'm not back before she gets hungry. And she's a sucker for zweiback, if you can order any from the kitchen."

Lore nodded warily, but her skin color seemed a little better when she turned to my dog, redness streaking the girl's cheeks as if she'd just walked outside on a wintry day. My collie came closer. But the prudish reserve drifted back into Lore Wylie's attitude when she looked up at me again.

"I'll take care of the dog," she said, and added formally, "Mr. Savage."

I nearly slammed the door back of me on the way out of there.

My pal Buzz Brennan, the columnist, was a tall and neatly dressed guy who had the successful man's habit of looking at something as if it didn't pay him to own it. Only when he was talking about the "out-and-out perverts" who read his daily gossip column did Buzz's face show a certain waspishness. Otherwise, from the top of his silver hair to the soles of his Haig and Haig shoes, he wouldn't easily get upset or irritated. His sense of humor was lively without ever being hurtful in the slightest.

Over lunch at the Paris-Soir I told him, "Buzz, I need some information about a crooked guy whose last name is Goodell."

"You got anything besides that? I may know about a lot of people, but I need more than a last name."

"The guy's in a dirty business, like I said."

"Um. Would you mean Nails Goodell? He steals laundry off washlines, but that's a pretty clean business."

"I'm laughing so hard, Buzz, I won't have much energy after I choke you."

"It could be Sherlock Goodell, couldn't it? A home builder. Had a big development out past Riverdale called Sherlock Homes."

"I don't believe that," I said, distracted.

"It's the honest truth, Mark. Years ago, this happened. The streets were named for characters in those fiction stories — you know? There was Watson Terrace and Baskerville Drive. But you want to hear the funniest bit of all? Sherlock was squeezed outta business by a syndicate headed by a fellow named Moriarty. A fact. Same name as the big villain in a lot of those stories."

"All right, it's a fact. Seriously now, do you know the guy *I'm* talking about? His name is pretty unusual."

"Seriously," Buzz said, and the twinkle faded out of his dark eyes, "I haven't got the slightest idea."

"I didn't want to tell you this much, Buzz, and I'm trusting you to keep quiet about it, but I think the guy is in the hot pictures racket."

"That changes things," Buzz said thoughtfully. "I'm not sure I ought to — well, let it go. Did you ever hear of a guy named Robert Goodell?"

"No."

"He used to be a big shot in his day, but he wasn't in crime. He was a movie cameraman, one of the artistic kind. Won a few Academy Awards, that's how good he was. Wouldn't have anything to do with the cheapola stuff you do stunt work in."

"He doesn't sound like a crook, so far."

"Well, things have changed for him. The story is that he pulled something so raw he was booted out of the business. Even the TV people won't have him, in fact. Goodell's not making money right now. If his bank balance is really shot, he might turn crooked, and I've heard some rumors that he's done it. Do you want to take a chance seeing him?"

"Write down his address and phone number."

Buzz grinned, nodded patiently and pulled out a small pad from a pocket. He wrote at an even speed that wouldn't have changed no matter what happened. He'd have dotted the last *i* if this restaurant had caught fire all around him.

"I sure hope he's the right one," Buzz said, after taking a leisurely sip of the Chateau Lafitte he had ordered. "It could be Ratface Goodell you're really after. He used to pimp for somebody he claimed was a bearded lady, but who was really a man. Or what about Jeb Stuart Goodell? He used to forge Confederate money and victimize curiosity stores — no? Well, I can see you're not in the mood for light conversation, stunt man. But you ought to take things a little easier, even if you do think I'm bugging you with those stories. Next thing I'll hear, you're going to be down in a hospital with ulcers or something weird like that."

## EIGHT

I stopped off at the Public Library on Fifth and Forty-second to check a reference book about movie makers. One of the green-and-white books I was shown held the information I wanted. Robert Goodell was a well-known cameraman with more than twenty experimental pictures to his credit, the kind that take a lot more knowhow than he'd have needed in grinding out a Western, for instance. No argument about one point, anyway: the man knew his business inside out.

The sun had turned even warmer than before, I realized on coming out of the library and hunting for a cab. It beat down so insistently my scalp tingled and all my clothes itched. The temperature was in the high 50's already, and I hoped it wouldn't go higher.

A Yellow Cab took me down Fifth to 23rd and followed Broadway into one of Greenwich Village's shabbier streets. The driver nearly exterminated a scrawny man with dead eyes who got out of the way just in time. Across the way a strutting boy put a soft white hand on each hip and laughed shrilly at the sight. He was hooting when I turned in hopes of finding the house I wanted to reach before the cab stopped in front of it.

A family clientele seemed to have been attracted to the brownstone museum piece just off Barrow where Robert Goodell lived. I passed some little girls playing hopscotch in the rubble-strewn courtyards as well as small boys keeping busy at tag or handball or what they referred to as "hango-seek." To reach the doorway I brushed past a couple of young women rocking baby carriages as they talked about food prices at the supermarkets.

I skip-stepped up a narrow hallway to the second floor. The doorbell was answered by a broad-shouldered guy in his early 50's. He was big all over as far as I could see, from the half-moon face to a pair of feet the size of bull-fiddles.

"What do you want?"

"Mr. Goodell, I want a little talk with you about movies."

His eyes looked me up and down as if he was judging from which angle I'd photograph best. It wouldn't have been surprising to hear a camera buzz at any minute now. I felt as if I'd been stuffed and mounted.

"I guess you can come in," he said finally. "Hell, what's there to lose?"

His brown loafers slapped the floor as he led me past a bare narrow foyer into a living room furnished with nothing more than a couple of broken-down couches, a cocktail table with one leg gone, and a dusty looking pole-lamp next to a dusty window. Goodell was almost certainly down on his luck.

"Well, what do you want?"

"A few minutes talk with you, Mr. Goodell."

"I can spare the time. My schedule isn't very full, these days. You can guess that much from looking around you."

"Everybody hits a bad streak once in a while."

"It's likely to last a long time for me," Goodell said heavily, "and I'd always figured movie making was a business you could grow old in. I came into movies years and years ago with 'Uncle' Carl Laemmle. That shows you how far back I go, doesn't it? As for TV, it's a youngster's business. Let's face it, anybody more than fifteen years old on either side of those dinky little cameras should have his head examined."

I didn't make any answer to that, let alone giving him the sympathy he craved. "You haven't asked me for my name yet, Mr. Goodell, but it's only fair that you should know it. My name is Mark Savage. I'm a private detective and I do most of my work for Hollywood people. Right now I'm on a job for an actress who claims she's been hurt in business on account of a 'hot' movie she says she never made."

"Too bad. I'm sorry to hear that. What makes you think I know anything about it?"

"I've been doing a job, Mr. Goodell. That means I've been checking around to ask questions. Don't you think I know plenty about the setup in filthy movies by this time?"

Impatience, as usual, made me edgy. This time it was the verbal sword-play in this dirty room with the huge, poverty-stricken, but competent, man that combined to make my nerves raw. I took a deep breath, let it out slowly and took another one while my heart ticked in furious reproof. Goodell sat thinking, eyes closed as he stroked his big jaw with oversized clumsy-looking hands. I felt my hair graying when he let out a sigh.

"I'll tell you this much, Savage," he said eventually. "Once a guy gets hungry, he'll dig pretty low for a buck."

"If you've photographed some dirt, say so."

"Back before I could grab a foothold in the movie business, I needed money very badly. Well, to make a long story short, some people came to me with a proposition. I wrestled my conscience for a while and finally agreed to do what they wanted. I photographed a filthy movie and collected a few hundred dollars for it. When I needed money again, I did another one. If I hadn't made those pictures at that time, Savage, I'd have starved."

That last part I couldn't believe. He might have landed dozens of honest jobs while waiting for the big break to come along. He had taken the easy way instead and now he was alibiing himself for what he'd done.

"I stopped doing it as soon as possible. My conscience bothered me for having degraded myself and I'd have given almost anything to have kept it from happening. The degradation was professional, too. The techniques were the shoddiest and worst, of course. The camera was a portable with a simple spring motor and a lumiere cam to move the film through. No dissolve scenes, no fadeouts."

"Forget all that part of it," I started to say.

"No, it helps prove the point of how much I hate it. The only way to photograph with that camera is at a blanket speed of 24 frames a second. There's no way of changing the speed. No slow motion, for instance, where you can shoot 48 frames to the second and show the actors moving at half normal speed. And you can't shoot a scene with an actor running and do it at fewer frames to the second so he seems to be running faster. You're trapped with that same damn speed all the time."

"Let's skip the technical part for now," I tried again when Goodell paused to take a breath.

"And then there's that awful lighting," he went on eagerly. "No arc lamps or gold-surfaced reflectors, nothing professional. Come to think of it, I'm amazed that they develop the film by reversal, which isn't a bad process, all things considered. The results don't come out grainy unless you enlarge."

"The worst thing *you* can say about 'art study' movies is that they're unprofessional," I put in sharply. "I've always thought that there are other bad things about them."

"Well, of course. Of course there are."

"But those things don't get you so excited as the bad photography does." Icily I added, "And I still don't believe you told every bit of the truth about those damned pictures."

"On my word of honor . . ."

"You're in a jam for money right now," I said, glancing around the shabby room one more time. "If you wrestled your conscience to a draw in the past, you can do it any time you want to. You know you'll make money by selling 'art study' movies. I wouldn't be surprised if you aren't back in business again, bigger and better than ever."

73

Goodell didn't finish what must have been a denial springing to his lips. The persistent sound of the doorbell ringing interrupted him. A finger had been jammed against the doorbell and was being kept there.

My host got up very quickly. His bull-fiddle sized feet took him into the foyer and out of my sight. I waited. The door was opened. The ringing stopped. I heard Goodell stepping back at the same time another man's footsteps came forward into the apartment.

A stranger said, "You know what I'm after, Goodell."

"Sure." Robert Goodell made his answer more quiet than necessary. "But let's not talk about it now."

"We'll talk about it," the stranger said roughly. His voice was hard and heavy. It could have trampled down anybody in the way without the owner making one move. "You wanted fifty grand for a certain piece of material. It's too much. A lot more than I'm willing to pay."

"That's my price," Goodell told him, "but, like I said, I don't want to talk right now."

"You can have ten grand for it, Goodell," the stranger snapped. "That's nothing to sneeze at."

"I'm not sneezing. I'm just not playing ball."

"You'll come around to it."

Suddenly there was a noise. Somebody had lashed out with a fist or a club and lashed out hard. I was already halfway out of my couch seat when it happened, a little surprised at having brought myself to wait that long. Now that the pressure was off me I took half a dozen steps to the foyer where I'd be able to see and talk to the man who was bargaining for what was almost certainly an "art study" movie before the powerfully built Goodell could smash him to pieces.

The sight that met me when I stepped into the foyer would have made anybody swear.

Two men were standing triumphantly at either side of Goodell. One of them whirled around to face me, pointing the 4-inch barrel of a blued-steel .22 Thunderbolt to my midsection at a range that could have cut me in half.

My narrowed eyes left the gun's snout and looked up vengefully. The guy who carried the Thunderbolt was more like a tiger than a dark-haired, five-foot-ten hood on the sunny side of forty. His gray brows were quirked in suspicion as he glared around him with quick motions, bobbing and ducking his head so that any trap wasn't going to find it in the same place as before. His nose crinkled when he drew a deep breath, as if not even the air in this room could be trusted worth a damn.

The second man was Ziggy, that ugly hatchet-faced messenger who had played hob with a side of my head over at Osterman's place. There was a blackjack in one of his hard hands, and a too-familiar wolfish smile seemed to have split his face as he looked down cheerfully.

Robert Goodell was on one knee and trying to get up. Just as he raised the knee Ziggy chuckled and leaned forward to kick him in the right side.

Goodell crashed down this time, hitting with a thud that jarred the furniture. Faint words escaped between his lips along with bubbly reddened spittle. He managed to raise his head an inch off the floor, then let it drop again.

"Keep an eye on him, Zig," the man holding the gun said. He was the one who had been talking to Goodell a minute ago. "For all I know, Goodell could be faking."

"He ain't, boss. I'll guarantee that."

"For all I know, any guarantee of yours isn't worth a damn. Do what I tell you and keep an eye on him."

"All right, boss, all right."

The boss threw a glance at Ziggy to make sure that the hood was obeying, then looked at me. The gun rose in his hands till a bullet coming out of it would have blasted my heart through a shoulderblade.

"Now who the hell are you?"

"That's what I was just going to ask you, pal."

"I know him, boss," Ziggy put in, pleasantly winded; after all a little light exercise never hurt anybody. "This goddamn snoop was in the place where I picked up some pictures. I told you all about it."

"What did you say his name was, Zig?"

"Savage."

"Yes, that's right, that's what you said. Did you tell me his first name, too?"

"Sure I did, boss. Mark Savage is his name, I told you."

"Uh-huh, Ziggy. That checks with what you told me before."

I glared at the boss. "And what does that do for you?"

"We'll get to it." The boss glanced down to

Goodell. "See if he's faking."

Ziggy opened the man's eyelids and let them shut. "Out like a light, Whit. Any time I hit somebody, he stays hit."

"Stand away from him, and watch this joker here for a minute. I'll look for myself."

Whit, the boss, waited till Ziggy was out of reach, then lifted the gun hand so that one could grab for it and bent down to check on Goodell's condition. He was much more thorough than Ziggy had been, but he was nodding reluctantly when he got up and pointed the gun at me again.

"That stupid bastard could have stopped it any time he wanted if he'd told me where the movie is. If you give me any trouble, you won't have it any better."

I watched his eyes flash from side to side and even above him, as if he was on the lookout for more booby traps. I wondered if he slept in a room that was guarded day and night. I also wondered if he used one of his men as a food taster to make absolutely sure that nobody was trying to spice his diet with some poison. I wondered if he insisted on having a woman examined for VD a few minutes before laying her.

"Ziggy," the boss said, making half a turn, "I'll get back soon, probably when you're not expecting me. Be careful here." With the .22 still thrust out at whatever might be in front of him, he walked into the living room. I heard two soft seats slashed with a knife. A mattress was cut from end to end in the bedroom, and stuffing scattered across the floor. Dishes and utensils were moved around in the kitchen. The insides of a medicine cabinet in the bathroom were scattered around and smashed. He wasn't likely to have skipped any possible place where a reel of movie film might be hidden.

I glared at Ziggy, telling myself how much I wanted to rip off one of those narrow feet and slam his thin face and thick, chunky body with it. When he saw me looking disdainfully at his shape, he let the blackjack whistle with menace in the air and then thud down into a beefy hand.

"Looking for trouble, sport?" he asked.

"From you, ugly? Don't make me laugh."

Ziggy dropped one hand to his side and raised the blackjack with his other hand. "I'll teach you who'se ugly, you bastard."

I was ready for him when he took a step forward. First I brought up one foot so that the tip of my shoe slammed into his belly. It doubled him up. I flattened a palm and chopped at the back of his neck. Ziggy let out a groan and fell across Goodell's unconscious form.

As I lifted a foot to give Ziggy a little more medicine, I heard the boss' hard-edged voice back of me: "Stop or I'll fill you with holes."

I stopped, turning toward him and the gun. He frisked me with his eyes.

"Empty your pockets and do it fast."

I controlled myself, but did it.

"Put your hands down and shake 'em so I can see what drops out of the sleeves . . . turn your cuffs down . . . open your mouth wide and spit . . . turn around and back. Okay, that settles it: there's nothing on you but your hands, and you didn't have time to stash a blackjack or brass knucks."

Ziggy groaned. The boss said angrily, "How the

hell is it possible for you to be carrying a blackjack and somebody else to ream you?"

"Boss, next time I'll get him good."

"So help me, Ziggy, I wouldn't be surprised if you sold me out and made some kind of a deal with this louse so he can get out of here and make you look like you were doing your job all the time."

"Deal? As soon as I get up, Whit, I'll show you what kind of a deal I make with him."

"Forget it now," Whit said after a keen look at his man. "I've got more important things to worry about."

"Okay, Whit, sure. It's forgotten — for now." But he was looking murderously at me.

The boss snapped, "Forget about fighting, I told you. I've got something more important to worry about. The movie I wanted hasn't turned up yet."

Ziggy furrowed his brow. "Well look, Whit, all we gotta do is wake Goodell and work him over again."

"So you can have a little more fun, huh? No, Goodell sounded too damn stubborn there. It wouldn't work."

"If you want to get anything, hit hard and heavy is what I say. Nothing else works as good."

"I have a strong hunch that something else might work, this time." The boss looked at me as if I were on display. "And the cards are played right, getting what I want can be pretty easy for me — now."

## NINE

Whit's little Thunderbolt persuaded me to leave the apartment with him and Ziggy. When we got to the street I asked him pointblank about what was on his mind, not being able to hold my curiosity any longer. Whit said he wouldn't broadcast it in the open air. Ziggy chuckled at the exchange and I told Ziggy I might make another hole in his face for him to laugh out of. Ziggy snarled and Whit, glancing feverishly around him at the near-emptied street, told both of us to quiet down and not make the beef a coast-to-coast business.

A black car was broiling under warm sun at the next corner, a huge sleek car that couldn't have been anything but a Cad. It was in perfect condition, as I could tell the minute Ziggy started driving. The pickup was smooth and the ride itself was like what you'd get on a moving cushion. The boss was never off-balance, keeping the gun pointed at me. There are people who have to strike gold in order to earn money, but this crew had made fortunes after panning for filth.

We drove down Christopher Street into 8th,

followed Lafayette to East Houston and made a right turn. This was a ratty section of the Lower East Side. Dirty gray buildings hovered on top of cheap looking stores. The best thing a member of the City Planning Commission could have done in this foul neighborhood was to root it up stone by stone.

There wasn't a store around us, however, that looked any shabbier than the one we stopped in front of. The Ace Bookshop, it was called. Its small dust-covered window showed magazines with sex in their titles and on the garish covers. The cheap hardbound books had titles like Visualizing the Nude. A tab in each book was marked: For Sale to Art Students Only. It must have been a wholesome business, all right. You could smell it in your nostrils before taking a step inside.

The boss, who'd been sitting ten feet away from me at the other end of the same seat, said to Ziggy, "Take him inside, Zig. I'll go in by the back."

At Ziggy's signal, I promptly got out of the car. I was curious to know where we were headed for and what those two men thought was going to happen once we all got there. It wouldn't bother me if they were disappointed.

The place was dirty in two senses of the word. Suggestiveness lurked in every dusty rack. Magazines with photographs of nudes on their covers were on display next to hardbound books wrapped in cellophane to prevent browsing. Every title I saw had the word "Sex" in it.

A clerk suddenly turned around to look at us. He was holding a duster in one thin hand, a small and scrawny guy in the 40's, with arms and legs like pipestems. He might have punched his way out of a paper bag with no trouble at all.

Ziggy told him, "We're going into the back."

"Suit yourselves," the clerk nodded, and managed to lift the duster a half inch above his head as he turned back to what he was doing.

I opened a small dark door and walked into a storeroom. Magazines were roped into bundles against three walls along with books in carton boxes. There was an out-of-use display sign against the fourth wall and a life-size mannequin of a nude woman with breasts like balloons.

Ziggy signalled me to knock on the deep-brown painted door.

"Savage?" the boss' voice asked, muffled.

"That's right."

"Come in alone. Zig, stick around out there."

As soon as I opened the door I blinked at the contrast between this place and the outside. It looked clean here and pretty rich, too. A wide, mahogany desk that isn't being given away with trading stamps was placed at the far end of the office. A costly zebra-striped couch had been set at one side along with a sturdy but comfortable-looking chair done in naugahyde. Dark velvety drapes sheathed the wide window at the far end. Coming into this place from its surroundings was like discovering Tiffany's in the middle of a garbage dump.

"Come in and sit down and relax," the boss said, nodding at me from his chair. "Better not make trouble for me in my own place."

"Why the hell not?"

"There'd be no sense in it. Lift a finger the

wrong way and I'll have Ziggy in here. And there's the gun, too. It's in the desk where I can get it easy."

"I didn't figure you'd let the gun out of your reach, but I'm surprised that you'd call Ziggy in here. I'd have been willing to bet good money you'd never let Ziggy into this palace. The outside ought to be good enough for him."

"Forget about the crap outside. It's a part of the front and I hate to walk through it myself. It shouldn't bother you."

"I feel better already."

"Don't get snotty, Savage. It'll make me harder to get along with. By the way, it's time we got organized. My name is White Kowler, and you ought to know it before we get to anything else. Does that name ring a bell with you?"

"It will, from now on."

"You're on guard, I'm on guard. Fair enough."

"I'm going to be on guard with a loaded cannon one of these days."

"You'd be knocking off a successful businessman if you fired it," Kowler snapped. "Savage, I have got to tell you one big thing about myself before we can go any further. I'm not going to enjoy this, but it's necessary. The fact is that I'm a pretty big guy at what I do. One of the biggest in the city. I own a hell of a lot of stores and I make money on magazines and books, too. Hell, I have the books printed up special."

"So you're a publisher, too?"

"I guess so, if you look at it like that. First I pay a writer for a good script. Then I pay an artist a hundred bucks for twelve illustrations and twenty-five bucks for the cover. I have a printing shop make photo-offset plates of the material. After the books are run off they're sent to the binders and then to a warehouse. Then they're packed up and sent to my retail stores in the city. On that one operation alone, believe it or not, my profit on every book is about five bucks on a printing of ninety thousand copies. Not bad, huh? And that's just one side of the over-all operation, the only side I'm going to tell you about."

"Probably because it's the 'honest' side," I said, my gut turning slightly as if I had just done an automobile roll on dry pavement. "You wouldn't talk to me about any other angle unless you were forced to; but I know without your telling me that filth always pays off."

"Don't try and protect the public morals, whatever you do." Kowler grinned. "I'm like anybody else, you know? I hate the people who might keep me from having a little pleasure."

"Who might smash this 'business' to pieces, you mean."

"I know that's what you want, now and I'll handle every move you make." He looked grim now. "Whoever's paying you to do it doesn't know what the score is."

"Nobody's paying me to bust your racket."

Kowler ignored that. "This business of mine ought to make money as long as there's one man who doesn't live a happy sex life and who needs some kind of a release, a substitute. He'll pay to be convinced that normal sex doesn't amount to much because all women are contemptible and they want to do some pretty vile things. He can adjust himself on account of what he buys from me. Without pornography, he'd go whole-hot batty."

"But you don't sound like you're dead certain about that, either," I said roughly. "You can skip the lectures."

"All I want you to realize is that I know my business inside out and I'm not a small-potatoes character," Kowler said. "But I'm not sure I know *your* business."

"Ziggy must have told you I do private eye work."

"Only in New York?"

"New York and California."

"Do you have any other line?"

His childish caution after having given me some information about himself nearly made me smile. "I've got a Screen Actors Guild card."

"The Hollywood connection gives you some advantage in dealing with Goodell," he said promptly. "You could talk to him as one insider to another and get something out of him."

"The stag movie? You want me to get hold of that movie and give it to you?"

"Uh-huh. And you know which one it is because you talked to Charlie Osterman about a movie with a certain famous actress in it."

"Kowler, you ought to keep away from heroin. You're not thinking too straight."

"I'll authorize you to buy the damn thing for as much as ten grand, provided you show me a receipt in Goodell's handwriting." He smiled cagily. "I'm willing to offer you more dough than it's worth to anybody else — and don't try to tell me there hasn't been an offer before mine."

With a catlike move he reached into a drawer, and one smooth hard hand came up with a folded batch of green bills. Gracefully he eased five of them down to the desk in a fan shape, pressing firmly at the apex of the fan in case I reached for it. His eyes held a tigerish gleam.

"Five grand don't sprout up on bushes, you know," he said finally. "You be where I can phone you every three hours because I want to know where you are and hear what you'll claim you're doing so I can make sure there's no additional trouble on top of everything else."

"I told you before —"

"Look here. You'll be treated just like anybody else who works for me, no better and no worse. I'd handle this personally, but I've got too many irons in the fire and I've got to check my men to see they aren't screwing up on the job. So what do you say?"

I looked at the fan of money on the desk and spat down toward it.

Kowler, chronically suspicious as he was, had pushed back the bills before my spittle could reach them. "Boy scout! Think you're going to impress me with that kind of foolishness, I suppose. How do you think I can believe anybody who acts like he's turning a chance at some good money for a job that doesn't take much work!"

Not trusting myself to say anything to him, I got up quietly.

"You may not go for the idea right now, Savage, but you're going to get around to it."

"How come you're so sure?" I asked finally.

"Because the money's good. A guy who has a lot of dough waved under his nose is somebody even I can almost trust to do what I want."

"You keep thinking that way," I said, "and we'll both be happy, if you know what I mean."

Ziggy glanced inquiringly into the office as soon as I opened the door to get out of there. He nodded at Kowler's signal to let me go, saying, "Okay, boss." With a hard hand, he gestured me to walk at one side, but he led the way back to the store entrance.

As we got there I suddenly stopped cold. What was going on looked so interesting in a morbid way that I couldn't keep from standing in one place to watch it. Ziggy didn't try to prod me into getting a move on. It would have brought him the kind of trouble he'd been ordered to keep away from. The two of us stood quietly.

The beanpole clerk was waiting on a customer. That thin welcoming smile he gave from his side of the dark wooden counter could have been completely covered by one of his bloodless looking pinkies. He was rubbing both hands together as if that warmth was what kept him going.

"How've you been, Mr. Hurst?" He asked the customer. "How was that last book? Good, huh? Now I suppose you want to sell it back for half the price. Fine, fine. I've got some books there that just came in, and they ought to interest a red-blooded man."

Mr. Hurst, the customer, a heavy-set fellow with a strawberry birthmark splotched down the left side of his face, picked out three books.

"By the way," the clerk said engagingly, wrapping them in plain brown paper, "have you left your name and address with us, Mr. Hurst? Sometimes I have to clear away merchandise, and I get rid of it very cheaply."

"Why should I leave my name and address in this place, for God's sake?"

"There are specialties besides books, you know, Mr. Hurst." The beanpole clerk was almost coy about it. "There are photographs."

"You don't need my name and address for those," the customer said. "Besides, you can't sell really good pictures, can you?"

"What you've got in mind is against the law, I'm afraid, Mr. Hurst. But the law could be stretched a little, if you follow me."

"I'm not a hundred percent sure that I do. You could — uh, sell certain pictures, is that it?"

"Well, you see, Mr. Hurst, if a checkup proved that you aren't connected with any undesirable people, then I might be able to stretch a point here and there."

"I see," Hurst nodded. "You've got the pictures, but you won't sell me anything that's really hot unless you're sure I can be trusted. Well, that puts a different angle on it, I suppose."

"More than that, Mr. Hurst. There are moving pictures, too, you know. Movies that are rented on a special arrangement."

"That's even better," Hurst nodded vigorously, rubbing the strawberry birthmark so that it was almost hidden by one big hand. "Yes, I'm interested all right. Where do I sign?"

I looked away, having already seen more than

enough to last me quite awhile. To last me forever. I nearly ran over to the door. No use kidding myself: I did feel sick clear down to the gut after all.

## TEN

Rex must have heard me walking along the floor to Lore Wylie's hospital room. My collie practically jumped at me as soon as I got inside. No wife ever welcomed a husband home so enthusiastically from a hard day's work. Before I disentangled myself my face was wet from forehead to chin.

Lore Wylie had been sitting up anxiously in bed, but sank down deep on seeing a man come in there, and pulled the blanket up to her chin. Then she shrugged, probably realizing that a visit like this one couldn't be helped. Her smooth white face searched mine for any good news that might just possibly be printed there. Or any news. She seemed to have stopped breathing till she'd find out.

"Have you got it?" she quavered. "That vile movie, I mean."

"I've made some progress."

"Can you prove that it was a double for me who was in that movie?"

"I'm not finished working yet."

"Oh." Her face fell, bringing some of her deep red hair down around both ears. "Then you haven't really done a thing except come in here prying on me."

"Lore, I'm doing every damn thing I can," I said tiredly. "I don't want you on my conscience."

"Maybe what you want is a few more chances to come into this room while I'm in bed," she snapped, tung at the tone of voice I'd taken. "That's what you're really after."

"You're a good looking woman, Lore, and you're a very successful actress, but I wouldn't want to jump in there next to you if I knew I'd earn a fortune out of it. I like a woman with some love in her, and that's the part somebody left out of you. I couldn't be sorrier about it, but I'd never hop into bed with a woman I feel sorry for . . . let me finish this. I know you're upset at the idea of an art movie turning up, but if you can't try slashing your wrists again till you're sent away from here, the least you can do is keep your mind off sex in the meantime."

"I've had enough of being insulted by somebody as lecherous as you are," she flared up. "You can drop the case right now. Any agreement between us isn't valid from now on."

"Lady, you're not the one who's paying me, and I'll keep at this mess till I've cleaned it up, whether you like my doing it or not. I'll come back when you've had a little while to consider that maybe I'm not trying to rape you after all."

I snapped my fingers, which brought Rex hurrying over to my side, and turned around promptly to the door. After taking a couple of steps in that direction, the door opened.

The girl who walked in was wearing a collarless black dress with tapered panels set in at the sides. She reached into a closet for a heavier coat than the weather called for, and smiled easily at Lore Wylie.

91

"Now that I have powdered my nose, as is the saying," she began, "I will be on the way, Lo — . . . ."

I cleared my throat. She looked at me with interest and I returned the compliment. Lore Wylie's friend couldn't have been more than five-eight, with velvety hair ending at a point in line with my chin. A tawny complexion adorned her heart-shaped face. When you get older you develop the habit of putting women into categories, and this one seemed like the kind of eager, emotional woman who belongs only in a warm climate. Dark and temperamental. She'd have stabbed a man for one peseta or given herself and all her money to another man if she liked the color of his eyes. I had already noticed that she had the graceful walk of a woman who'd spent a lot of time carrying baskets on her head while strolling through the marketplace in a tropical village.

"This is Miss Gomez," Lore Wylie said coldly when I had been gazing for a while. "Miss Maria Gomez."

"It's a pleasure," I said honestly.

"The same here, chico." If her voice hadn't been warm and sultry I'd have lost all faith in women. "Chico, you are handsome man."

"I've got some other good points, too," I began solemnly.

The door opened swiftly on a fat old nurse in a rush. She waddled over urgently to stand at the side of Lore Wylie's bed and cleared her throat.

"There's an important phone call for you, Miss Wylie," she said. "A man who claims he's got something to tell you and it's practically life and death. A Mr. Robert Goodell."

My head jerked sharply to the right, where Lore Wylie looked up at me out of blue eyes fully as cold as the rest of her.

"Aren't you leaving, now that you've made a new friend?"

I glared from her to the nurse. The nurse's thumb darted to a point in front of the emergency bell. I drew a deep breath and forced myself to look back and smile slightly.

"Chico." It was Maria Gomez. "If you are leaving, too, perhaps you can give me a lift to your hotel."

"Sure, sure," I said negligently, frustration on account of work keeping me from any consideration of my chances with this beauty. "If you want to."

For once I dragged my feet getting away from someplace.

"Brrr!" Maria drew the hip-length short coat tightly around her in spite of the warm weather, squeezing raglan sleeves with her fingers as if she wanted to force extra warmth out of them. "The winter is terrible time in New York."

Maria dropped a white-gloved hand on my arm and kept it there while I hailed a cab and helped her inside. She moved close to me when I got in with Rex, but moved away when Rex growled. My collie didn't have much use for the girl. Sex jealousy, I was sure.

"The dog does not like me," Maria said placidly. "It is the temperament, chico. Mine. I am very,

very emotional."

"I hope so," I smiled, giving her my full attention. "Would you have any idea what that life-and-death phone call to Lore might be about?"

"Probably it is not important." She shrugged. "In this business, everyone gets excited over a crisis that will not last long. I am that way, too, perhaps worse than most."

"You're an actress?"

"*Si.* The Spanish types are very popular now, but only for supporting roles. Their appearance brings in many Puerto Ricans to see cheap films."

I had never heard of her. The technical people in my branch of the business look down their long noses at the so-called creative gals and guys, and practically make a hobby out of not knowing their names.

"When you find out anything about the phone call Lore just had," I told her, "I'd appreciate hearing it."

"*I* am in no hurry to ask." She had switched moods for only a little while, I was certain, becoming distant and apparently unconcerned. "Besides, I may not see you again during my three days in this city."

"Sure you will," I nodded agreeably. "Three days, huh? That'll be enough time for me to find out about you."

"Find out what, chico?"

"Everything," I grinned, and suddenly needled her. "About the accent, for instance. I'd like to know if anything so thick is completely phony or only a small part of it is put on."

Maria Gomez didn't take kindly to any needling.

94

She called out, "Pig! American pig! *Norteamericano* pig!" and made a fist.

I slapped her. Maria gasped, then subsided and sat back. Rex would've lunged at her if I hadn't gestured the dog to be still. Having cursed my ancestry, Maria cried softly to get pity from me. All women write their own rules and change them as they go along. It's a waste of time trying to understand them; just keep on your toes and react swiftly at all times.

"Let's face it, Rex," I said a few hours later while sitting at the pine table in my kitchen and eating a steak hot off the broiler along with french fries, "I'm still doing a job for Lore Wylie."

Rex looked up from her dinner. She's always attentive if I say anything at mealtimes. That's part of my reward for not reading a newspaper while we eat. Rex is feminine enough not to have any tolerance for that, so the two of us have got a deal going.

"She lost her temper at me — Lore Wylie, I mean, not your friend Maria — but that's not the end of it. I won't have Lore Wylie's misery on my conscience. A man has to draw the line somewhere."

Rex nodded the first time I paused.

"And there's the fee, of course," I went on. "That kind of money is nothing to sneeze at. After all, why should I expect to pick up the money as if earning it was the easiest thing in the world?"

Rex was still listening, but she glanced down longingly at the contents of the blue bowl with dinner in it. Her heart was with chopped liver just then, not business talk. This was the time of night when she bolted her food.

I smiled as I stood up and tapped her on the rump before walking into the living room and reaching out for the phone. I told the operator that I wanted to put through a long distance, person-to-person call to Mr. Jules Schlosser, Executive Vice President in charge of production at Globe Studios in Hollywood. The operator said that she'd try to reach Mr. Schlosser as soon as possible. I hoped she'd get to him before the month was out, but I didn't say so.

She ran Schlosser to earth half an hour later out at a golf club somewhere. His jovial voice boomed agreeably into my ear in that standard Southern California sunshine tone that they grow out there along with oranges. He's have automatically called Jack the Ripper "sweetheart" if the two of them had been casual acquaintances.

"Hello, passion flower," he said. "What's the weather in New York?"

"Warm for winter."

"Well, we're in a goddamn cold spell out here. Worst thing in the world to play golf when it's cold, passion flower."

"Cut out the romance, Jules, will you? I get hot just listening."

"Okay, sweetheart, don't razz me. What can I do you for?"

"It's not too easy for me to explain, but I'll make it as short as possible. What I want you to do is to authorize me to hire an experienced man to work in a movie for you. A cameraman named Robert Goodell."

"Him? Why, I wouldn't hire that ticked-up handkerchief-head if my life depended on it. Of all the rank bastards, he's number one."

"What did he do to you?"

"Well, I won't mention names on the phone, but the guts of it is that he tried to extort money from one of the top people at Zenith studios. He's blacklisted, so we can't go near him — or at least we aren't supposed to."

"I knew he was on the nit list, Jules. Even if somebody hadn't told me about it, I'd figure that a guy with as many credits as he's got would land work, no matter how few pictures the studios are shooting."

"Look here," Schlosser's voice suddenly grew sharp. "What I told you is between friends. I don't want you passing it around."

"Of course not, Jules. Besides, everybody knows that there isn't any blacklisting in Hollywood. All those stories are Russian propaganda."

"Knock it off, will you? I was forgetting what kind of a notty, lippy soul you could be, sweetheart, even on the cross-country tube."

"When you get back to talking English again," I said mildly, "let me know."

"Goddammit, don't turn cute on me! All I want you to do keep what I told you to yourself."

"Don't worry about it. Here's something that might make you change your mind about hiring Goodell. You know I've been doing some work for . . ."

"Don't mention her name," he cut in frantically. "No names on the tube, whatever you do. How the hell do we know who could be listening?"

"All right. I've been doing some work for one of your people. She and I had a bust-up not too long ago, but it's temporary as far as I'm concerned. I've got to finish the job, and this favor I want from you is part of it."

"I ought to have known. Okay, big boy, you can offer that crum a spot out here if you *have* to — hey, wait! How serious is this about — her? You know, the one you're doing the job for."

"Pretty serious."

"Is there any chance of truble? If there could be even a sniff of bad publicity, tell me right away and I can start unloading her."

"You're a real good friend to the people who work for you, Jules. Loyalty like that is something a woman can't buy without money."

"This is a matter of business, goddamit! Everybody in this town has got an ironclad contract you could drive a tank through, and you know it as well as I do."

"All right, all right, I think this mess is going to work out the right way."

"You think? For God's sweet sake, is that the best you can tell me when the studio's got so much money involved?"

I snapped, "So long, Jules."

"No wait, wait. Keep in touch, will you? Promise me you'll keep in touch and pass the word in case we have to ditch you-know-who."

I hung up quickly, and drew a long angry breath. A blind man in the movie industry would need to have grossed plenty on his most recent picture before anybody out there was likely to help him cross the street.

## ELEVEN

I got my rented, coffee-colored Renault out of the building garage after dinner and, sitting almost at the edge of the driver's seat, began heading out to Goodell's place. With hard-won skill, I cut through traffic that threatened to hold me up and dodged a couple of red lights, at least.

"I hope our man's home by now," I said to Rex, who was at my side and looking attentively at the night-fogged scenery. "I phoned a couple of times for an appointment, but damned if I got any answer, and I don't feel like waiting around for him."

Rex admonished me with her eyes as the Renault squeaked out from between a Cad and a Rambler, missing two pedestrians by inches.

"I'm going to lay it on the line to Goodell and say that he'll get a movie job provided I get that stag film back. What's more I'll tell him that if any prints of it turn up he'll be through for good. I won't make that offer twice, and if he doesn't take it the first time I may wring his damn neck just to prove it."

A parking space loomed only half a block from the brownstone that Goodell lived in. Rex pouted when I got out of the car alone, so I gestured her offhandedly to come with me. The two of us walked into the building and past a toothless old man in a battered straw hat. He glanced at us, shrugged to himself and walked out.

There was no answer when I rang Goodell's doorbell on the second floor. I rang half a dozen times, louder and longer each time. Nothing. I knocked vigorously, getting no response from Goodell, but the door itself gave way very slightly; it was unlocked. I swore at Goodell for having kept me waiting.

Rex growled an inquiry. I pursed my lips in disapproval, not wanting her to throw a tantrum and foul up the works so that I'd have to play nursemaid to her.

"Down, girl!" I snapped. "Sit!"

With a certain ladylike disdain she did what she was told.

I took a quick step inside, found a pimple-sized light switch and flicked it on. Under a pudgy bulb bearing copper filament, the foyer burned yellow. One look along it and I stopped. Small icy waves lashed the underside of my spine.

Somebody in a frenzy had stabbed Robert Goodell again and again, and left him on his back in almost the same position as after the beating he'd taken on account of White Kowler. Blood had been spattered over his rumpled and ripped clothes and had dried, highlighting the ten or fifteen punctures that must have been made with the brown-handled fruit knife still sticking in him.

Considering that Goodell's actions had driven at least one woman to try suicide, I wasn't able to feel sorry about what had happened to him. His long overdue death was the killer's tragedy, not

Goodell's at all.

In another way it was Lore Wylie's tragedy, too. I now had as little chance as ever before of getting the prints of that "art study" movie she was supposed to have appeared in. My ace-in-the-hole wasn't worth a nickel any more.

Rex growled outside, probably at a small noise not too far away. She reminded me, though, that if I wasted time here, the cops might arrive at any second and start scraping pieces off the hide of their number one suspect, a stunt man and part time private operator named Mark Savage. The less they knew about me, the better I'd feel.

I pulled out a handkerchief and swiped it around the walls as fast as I could, hurriedly obliterating any prints I might have made. Still using the handkerchief I flicked the light shut, got the door opened as fast as possible, took a few running steps out, and then snapped the door closed. By sweeping my hand in half a circle I motioned Rex to get moving with me.

And on the ground floor level I nearly crashed into a uniformed cop.

It happened because there wasn't too much room for walking by, and he was in conference with another man whose features I couldn't make out in the dimness. Nobody showed any sign of stepping back an inch to let Rex and me through. Something had to give.

"Watch it," the cop said when I bumped into him. He whirled around alertly, a sharp-eyed youngster standing very stiff in what was probably his first uniform. He looked ready to hang up a record of cautions to passing citizens that would be a model for the whole department. "Watch where you're going."

"Sure, sure."

"You look nervous," he said to me.

"I'm all right."

"When a man gets jumpy, the rules tell me to wonder why," the cop said, not so politely this time. "What's your business here?"

"I live in the building."

Back of the cop a voice said clearly, "That ain't true."

I looked around and made out a toothless old man in a battered straw hat. I'd noticed him on my way inside. He had looked at Rex and me without saying a word. A nice old codger, I had figured him for. Well, next time I saw an old man looking after the two of us I'd automatically be expecting the roof to fall in a little later.

"This guy got into the building a few minutes ago, him and this dog." The old man spoke very clearly, considering that there wasn't one tooth between his gums. "I never seen him before and I know everybody who lives here. I'm what you might call a snoop."

The young cop's eyes showed flinty sparks when he looked at me again. "How come the lie, mister?"

"Maybe your friend's eyesight needs improving," I said. "Maybe he doesn't know that I moved in here only a few days back."

"We can settle it soon enough," the cop said to me. "Let's go up to your apartment."

"I suppose we *can* do that," I nodded, dredging up a smile out of nowhere. "But I'm in a hurry right now and as far as I see, all I've done that's wrong is to bump into you. I'm sorry it happened; but that's not enough reason for giving me the third degree, is it?"

"Let me have a look at your wallet," the young cop said, calmly walking over in front of the door so that I couldn't make a run for it in that direction. "It's enough to prove what you're saying. It'll have your name and address inside."

That was part of the trouble. The young cop was sure to write them down, and he'd haul the notebook out later on when Goodell's dead body was found. In less than no time after that, detectives would be sniffing around me with questions. And they wouldn't let go till I was wrung dry and not able to get any work done for Lore Wylie. Detectives enjoy nothing better than tripping up any man who is out to do a job that they feel they ought to be handling themselves.

There was one chance for me to get out of this. I suddenly looked at ease and shrugged as if I was helpless. "All right, you've been too smart for me. I'll have to tell you the truth. I don't live here. I have a house in Syosset on the Island. I'm a businessman, in ball-bearings. I've got a good factory, a wife and two lovely kids if I do say so myself. But the truth is . . . ."

My head was down almost on top of my chest, so that I seemed to be talking directly to my navel. At least the rules-conscious young cop wouldn't see my face if I wasn't able to keep it straight and unsmiling.

"I don't know what got into me, officer. Kind of a lunacy, a nuttiness. A man can be happily married, like I say, with everything to live for, and then he does something foolish on account of a pretty face and a good young body."

"You mean you've got a girl living here?"

"I'm ashamed to say so, but it's true. We stay together sometimes, and I drive by whenever I can. Once in a while I bring the dog with me."

The cop seemed a little more friendly because he was starting to feel some contempt for me. "You married men, you're all alike. A cousin of mine, he got mixed up in that kind of monkey business. Then he swore to his wife that it'd never happen again. A few months later he knocked up a secretary who worked in his office."

I sighed.. "Well, I'm going to give this girl up, officer. I've decided on that now. There's no sense torturing myself. This has been a lesson to me."

"A guy who's married can still look around if he wants, but it's no good touching the merchandise, believe me," the young cop advised me solemnly. "I'm telling you this for your own sake."

It looked like I had turned the trick. This kid would probably lecture me in the best Dutch uncle style and forget to follow up on what I'd been doing. But the toothless old guy had been stirring restlessly. Now he gave an amphatic shake of thyhead and cleared his throat with the impatient rumble of a bowling ball streaking down an alley.

"Ain't true what he's sayin'," the toothless wonder put in. "I seen him go up only a few minutes back, and I couldn't help wonderin' which apartment he was on the way to. Like I told you before, I'm a snoop. I like to know everything. So I walked upstairs slow and cautious, and there was the dog standing in front of somebody's apartment

104

and guarding it."

This was a pain in the rear end, for sure. His story must have been true. The toothless joker had shambled up the stairs for a look around. The proof of it had been in Rex's behavior. I'd heard her growling very faintly at one time while I was inside Goodell's place. Now I knew the reason for it.

"I figured you must be a burglar who used the dog for a lookout," the toothless guy said to me. "So I did my duty as a citizen and called a policeman. That's why you're having so much trouble getting away right now, bud."

"This is ridiculous," I said. "It's true that sometimes I leave my dog in front of the apartment when I go inside. I do it when I'm not figuring on staying for long. That doesn't mean I'm a burglar."

"There's no woman living in 2C," the old duck said. "That's the apartment I saw this mutt in front of."

"I never went into *that* apartment," I told him promptly. "You're dead wrong about the number."

The cop looked from one of us to the other and made a decision. "We have to settle it," he said. "The rules say so, and common sense does, too."

"I'm not going to have my girl friend pestered," I said, trying to sound firm about it. "After all, this kind of arrangement is hard enough on her without her having to be treated like a criminal."

"Get one thing straight." The cop pointed a thin forefinger between my eyes. "We're going to follow this thing to the finish, like the rules say.

Don't get any different ideas. We'll start by going up to apartment 2C for a look around. You go first."

There wasn't any help for it. Taking hold of Rex by the shortest lead I could manage, I turned her around to face the dim-lit stairs a second time. We walked back up, the cop coming determinedly behind us. The toothless man's malicious senile laughter had faded into the distance by the time we reached the second floor.

The cop gestured me roughly to stand aside aside, then rang the doorbell a couple of times. He knocked. He tried the knob. The door opened. He glared back at Rex and me and drew his gun out with purposeful slowness.

"Don't even scratch an eyebrow, mister," he said, "or I'll be after you. My ears are damn good, and so's my shooting."

The cop took a step inside. Light drenched the foyer and he looked its length. He stiffened, and his face turned darkly belligerent as he pounded out of there and stood directly in front of me.

"A girl friend, huh?"

His fist had power behind it. Flames exploded inside me and swept my whole body as I doubled up helplessly.

## TWELVE

The police station was one of those four-walled antiques that the City of New York preserves as a public building. Anything inside it that isn't at least a hundred years old is about ninety-nine and three-quarters.

It was my second time in this place tonight. I'd been given permission after gabfest number one to take Rex back to my apartment and put her to bed. She had tried to gnaw the arresting officer to shreds, and had snarled while my name and address were taken, my pockets emptied and a preliminary statement put down. There'd been no other sensible way of getting her out of all our hair. I had been accompanied on the short trip by a plainclothesman, of course. Now I was back for more questioning.

I sat in an office just big enough for a window, a desk, and three chairs. The empty one would do fine for a stenographer later on, I supposed. Opposite me was a police lieutenant back of his desk slopping over the chair he was on. Arnold Jessup was a heavy, horse-faced, graying man who carried his two hundred pounds with all the dignity of a seal balancing a rubber ball at the end of its nose. He was a slow-moving man who took a week to examine the written statement I'd already made and another month before looking me full in the face. After enough of that to satisfy a portrait painter, he started the question period.

"Is there any fact you'd like to tell me aside from what you've already said, Savage?"

"I can't think of a single one."

"Like, for instance, why you made such a mess of the dead man's place. What were you searching for?"

"I didn't do that, Lieutenant. I've said so, before. What I'd like to know is whether I'm under arrest or not."

"All I can say right now is that you're a material witness." He sighed as if it hurt to commit himself about anything at all. "Your story is that you've been doing work for somebody whose name you won't give, but that the customer couldn't possibly have killed this man Goodell. And you want me to take your word for it. Right?"

"More or less. And I don't think you can prove differently, Lieutenant."

"It looks that way. If a guy on the job I've got isn't able to prove what he thinks, then he's really up the creek without a paddle."

"So I can leave, I guess.

"No dice on that, Savage. You're holding out on the main points, though you've been sharp enough to give us as much of the true story as you can tell, I'm sure. And it's a very bad thing for you. You can't legally say that your customer's name and what he said to you are privileged communications. Only a lawyer can get away with that, and you're not a lawyer."

"So you're going to keep me around."

"It stands to reason." Jessup drew a Camel inch

by inch out of the pack on his desk, tapped both ends against an edge and lit the far end slowly. The flame wasn't more than a whisker's length away from one fingernail when he blew out the match. "Maybe you'll tell me something before your social security comes due, if you're in the cooler long enough."

"What I'll tell you, Lieutenant, will hardly be fit for human ears."

"I've heard that kind of stuff before," Jessup nodded. "But you won't like being kept incommunicado by getting shuffled around from one station house to another. Maybe you'll even get a workover every hour on the hour if somebody near you doesn't like the way you talk. In time you'd start telling what I want to hear, Savage. Time is on the law's side."

"Oh I'd *talk*, Lieutenant, but what I'd say is something nobody'd enjoy hearing. Besides I know perfectly well that if I ever give away the name of somebody I'm working for, my business as a private eye will be shot to pieces. That's something I won't let happen, no matter who I have to clobber first. I mean that, Lieutenant."

"We may need to find out if you've actually got a choice any more, Savage. But I'm willing to be fair about this if you can give me one sensible reason why I should let you out of here, instead. One will be enough."

"Because I didn't kill Goodell and I don't know a damn thing about who did." I took a deep breath and a solid guess in that order. "I'm pretty sure a post-mortem report will prove Goodell was knifed hours before I came to the place. His blood was

109

dried when I saw him, and when the cop who brought me in looked at the body a few minutes later. That's proof I didn't do the job in the time I was up there."

"You could have been to Goodell's apartment earlier in the day and stabbed him about fifteen times."

"What kind of a shlockhead would come back to a place he'd done a kill at?" I snapped. "And you couldn't make a jury believe it had happened that way in a million years."

"I could try," Jessup said grimly. "I'm starting to think I ought to, even though I generally hate to make a decision that fast."

"You're real conscientious, Lieutenant — like hell!" I wasn't in the mood for getting into his good graces. "I ought to duck your head down into a spittoon, but it doesn't make sense for me to do that."

Jessup said very quietly, "I suppose you know I really can slap you silly for a remark like that."

"What in hell's stopping you, then?"

"Oh, I've got a reason that might just possibly interest you, Savage. It goes back to something I did years ago, when I was a young cop on night duty. I saw somebody crawling out of a warehouse window by moonlight and shouted to him to stop or I'd shoot. He didn't stop, so I fired two times. He fell. When I got to him he was dying. He called out for his mom as I bent over him. He was a kid of about fourteen, already grown up to man-size. I'd stopped a heist artist all right, but I didn't really have to do the first thing that popped into my head. Shooting him down was wrong, it was horribly wrong. A departmental hearing exonherated me, but my conscience never did."

"That's too bad," I said sincerely. "A rough break for anybody."

"What I've been trying to tell you, Savage, is that I've made it a rule ever since then to go slow on the job and off, whenever I could. You can thank the memory of a dead kid that you aren't getting the personal workover you put yourself in line for."

He hadn't looked at me once in the last few minutes. After calling a uniformed man into the office, Jessup ordered, "Take my lippy friend here to a detention cell till I get ready for him."

"Yes, sir."

I didn't say one word to him. Maybe it was true that I had done too much talking before. One of these days my temper would be sure to land me in a very bad mess if I didn't learn to control it. But I doubted that I'd ever learn. Even if I had to live on tranquilizer pills for the next ninety years, I'd be a blowtop every day of that time.

A half mile walk with no tourist attractions worth mentioning brought me to a row of small cells. The cops graciously allowed me to stay in one. It would have taken a guy with cast-iron nerves to get any sleep at all, so I tried to figure out another way of goosing time. I walked calmly to one end of the cell, then walked back. I measured the place as carefully as if a big contract depended on it.

A cop showed up to take me out of there just as

I was getting ready to try pulling it to pieces. Gray streaks flared in the night sky as I walked back into the lieutenant's office again. Jessup was setting a cigarette on fire with that lightning speed of his and nodding his head patiently over a report on the desk. Looking up at me took him half an hour, as usual. It seemed as if he hadn't moved an inch in any direction since last time.

"Well?" he asked finally. "Changed your mind about talking sense to me?"

"No."

"At least you've got brains enough to answer a question yes or no. There are plenty of knuckleheads around who can't even do that much. I suppose you realize that leaving the scene of a crime and not reporting it to a police officer, which is what you're positively guilty of, happens to be a misdemeanor. You can be brought into court for that and given a few days in the jug."

"I realize it."

"But I've talked to the Assistant DA on this case, and he feels that the jug is crowded enough already, and that it's a sweaty business trying to get information out of a joker who won't be made to talk. Besides, the post-mortem report proves you didn't kill Robert Goodell during the only time you're known to have been in the apartment. Goodell had already been dead for hours."

"Does that mean you're letting me go?"

"That's what it means all right, Savage."

"Thank you, Lieutenant. I'm glad to hear it."

I looked as glad as if I didn't know what was really on Jessup's mind. He'd have me followed till I tipped off as much information as he wanted and then he'd drop the net around me again as a material witness. That was Standard Operating Procedure on certain cases. Tell every canary that the cage is really open and see what the stupid bird is up to.

"I'm doing my job straight, that's all, and a cop who does is poison to the rest of the world. Well, that means nothing to you, Savage. You can get out."

"There's one more thing, Lieutenant," I said quietly. "It's about a certain remark I made to you last time. Maybe I was rude and boorish, I honestly don't know. I'm still too close to it to be sure. But if I was, I'm sorry."

"You want to hear something, Savage?" A look of surprise crossed Jessup's fat face. "I've been back of this same desk more than ten years and this is the very first time a suspect ever apologized to me. Christ! If the whole world came to an end tomorrow, I wouldn't be shocked after this. It would be an anticlimax, so help me!"

He still looked dazed when I started out of the office.

## THIRTEEN

Rex was standing in front of the cabinet where I kept the stiff-bristled brush with which I groomed her every day. I gave her half an hour's treatment after breakfast, alternating the brush with a steel comb whenever I got to tangles. Rex looked so regretful once the fun was over I washed her eyes with boric acid and cleaned the insides of her ear flaps with a soft wet cloth. She started to whimper when she saw me putting the beauty kit away, but I told her firmly that she'd had it for now and that I'd had it, too.

My agent phoned long distance a little later on to ask if I'd do a ninety foot dive off a cliff into six feet of water for a picture being shot in Vermont. I told the agent I could use a thousand dollar fee as much as anybody and I'd done the stunt two times in the past, so I would be out there by the end of next week. Skullbusters like that one are ten times trickier than hell, but there's no feeling like the pleasure you get after a "walk through" when you do it thoroughly and right. By the end of next week, I hoped, this business with Lore Wylie would have been completely cleared up. Otherwise I didn't know just how I'd be able to stomach New York City after all that time.

I turned on the radio to a station that featured "classical jazz" and hurriedly got dressed to Duke Ellington's *Take the "A" Train*. I made up my mind how to ditch the detectives who must be all set to shadow me till further notice.

When I got outside to another warm day I signalled for a cab and was taken to the subway station at 77th Street. As doors started to close on the train that had come along, I barely squeaked inside at the last possible moment.

For insurance's sake alone I did a repeat on a Lexington Avenue Express at Forty-second.

After getting out at Thirty-fourth I took a cab crosstown and told the driver I'd give him an extra five dollars if he got to the Dutch County Hospital in ten minutes; I'd already been delayed long enough. The driver battled through downtown traffic, but he didn't earn that extra fin.

The starchy graying woman back of the reception desk at Dutch County seemed to lose all her frozen dignity for once when she saw me. She swallowed a couple of times and looked embarrassed. Redness flowed up the column of her long neck as I walked over to her.

"I'm awfully sorry, sir, but you can't see Miss Wylie."

"We've had this argument before, if you remember, and I won it last time."

"No, you don't understand. I'd let you up if Miss Wylie was in her room, but she's not there. Miss Wylie's gone. She's disappeared."

"What the hell!" I warned myself not to throw a wingding now, and swallowed black bile instead. "How did it happen?"

"Well, I really shouldn't gossip . . ."

I gritted my teeth. "As a friend of Miss Wylie's, I can't help wondering about it."

"Yes, of course. Well, it seems that Miss Wylie had a visit from another friend of hers, a Miss Gomez. I believe *she* acts, too — one of those 'Spanish' types, she sounds like, but I don't believe it somehow."

I nodded tautly. I hadn't quite believed Maria Gomez was a genuine Latin either, but that didn't make any difference now.

"Well," the receptionist continued, "it seems that Miss Gomez left and then — why, I swore I saw her leaving again. Of course I asked her what it was all about and she told me how it had been done."

"Do you mind telling me?" I asked very carefully.

"Miss Gomez had brought an extra coat, a dress and gloves, and a wide-brimmed hat. She had worn two outfits. Miss Wylie took one of them, and put on a lot of dark make-up to change her skin color, and she left first."

"Do you know why she did it?"

"No, I don't, and neither did Miss Gomez know when I asked her." The receptionist sighed. "That woman, Miss Gomez, she said she herself didn't mind playing hell with the rules of what she called a *yanqui* hospital. Those Spanish or Latins, whatever you call them, they're like children."

"What time did Miss Wylie pull her getaway?"

"At about half-past four yesterday afternoon."

I nodded. That wasn't too long after she'd talked on the phone to Goodell. Pictures rose in my mind of Lore Wylie quitting this place and buying a package of razor blades and, at the hint of being mixed up in a scandal whether she was innocent or not, slowly and carefully cutting her wrists.

"I can't understand what's got into this place," the receptionist was saying. "We used to be so conservative about the people we'd let in here . . . and no gentleman ever turns his back on a lady! At least you could say goodbye. A little manners never hurt. We used to be so conservative here, so refined!"

Doctor Leonard Bogen was one of those medical men who make a good living mainly because their manners inspire confidence. His deep mature voice and the pleasant smile that could widen into a happy grin, and even the dusting of gray at his temples were sure to keep him off the welfare roles forever.

Doctor Bogen had agreed to see me right away because I had sent in a note with his nurse saying that it was about his patient, Lore Wylie, and that it was urgent. Less than a minute after I had written out the note, his nurse was hustling me past a seated double-row of patients in the waiting room.

Bogen sat looking carefully up at me — he was a six-footer, I guessed, so he didn't have to strain too much. He nodded his relief when I told him I was the one who had phoned him a few nights ago to ask for permission to visit Lore. At least I was somebody the patient knew, very likely a close friend. He waited, encouraged, to hear me speak my piece.

"I want a little information from you, doctor. Do you have any notion where Miss Wylie is?"

"Not any," he boomed, hiding his disappointment as he paused to light a fresh cigarette from an old one. "I wanted Lore Wylie in the hospital where she could be watched. I didn't want here out of there."

"Would she have the use of her hands now?"

"Definitely. The wounds she made on herself when she attempted what she did were very shallow. Frankly, Mr. Savage, I was keeping her in bandages at Dutch County mainly because I wanted her under observation and out of police hands."

"Is there any chance that she committed suicide, doctor, or that she figures on doing it?"

"Let's hope not."

"Do you know any reasons why she wouldn't do it?"

"All I can think of is that she wasn't overly depressed the last time I saw her. It could mean one thng or the other, of course. No, Mr. Savage, I don't know."

"That leaves two of us up in the air."

"Completely, I'm afraid. You're looking disgruntled, Mr. Savage. Did you think I'd have all the answers? Do you have the charming idea that a man with a medical degree knows everything?"

"It just about crossed my mind," I said ruefully.

"Well, I'm as foolish as most people. There are things I don't know, and I can't help doing what's wrong about some of the things that I do know." He held up the lighted cigarette as if it was a small snake. "I can't cut out smoking, for instance, though I've got reason to believe that it'll shorten my life span. Overworking won't do me any good, either, but I keep spending ten hours a day seeing people who are desperately anxious to be a little sick."

I stood up. "Thanks anyhow, doctor."

"Sorry I couldn't be more helpful."

"I'm sorry, too."

As soon as I planted a fat row of dimes on the ledge of the nearest phone booth, I went to work, reducing the stack. I made quite a dent in it before getting finished. There couldn't have been more than half a dozen left by that time.

A call to the Beckwin Hotel desk brought me the news that Miss Wylie was still registered, but she hadn't shown up lately and her clothes hadn't been touched or moved. Nothing at all seemed to have changed in those people's relations with Lore Wylie since she'd been taken to Dutch County hospital.

Maria Gomez had been staying at the Beckwin, too, near her friend, Lore. Maria had checked out. The senorita had done "el scrammo" out of the *norteamericano* hotel late yesterday afternoon, saying that she was on her way back home to California. The clerk didn't have any reason not to believe her. Neither did I.

Harold Radfield was gone, too, according to the clerk at the hotel where Lore's business manager had been staying.

It was a clean sweep, all right. By way of checking up on everything I'd heard, I put through a call to Buzz Brennan, interrupting my old buddy halfway through the next day's gossip column. He told me he was using the item that La Gomez had left for California, and he understood Harold Radfield was gone too. He was still sitting on the L.W. yarn, as he'd been asked to do. If I had any info, would I let him have it exclusive? The readers of his column, those mewling, snail-brained perverts would eat it up raw when he released the story. I told Buzz not to worry about getting cooperation from me.

I called my New York City answering service next. A saccharine voice at the other end told me that a Mr. Kowler had called seven times and had asked me to phone back right away. No, Mr. Kowler had phoned eight times, actually, and had accused the answering service of lying to him just before cutting the connection furiously.

Whit Kowler was his usual suspicious self when I reached him at the Ace Bookshop. "You've been going behind my back, Savage, and trying to get that stuff, huh?"

"What are you talking about?"

"Never the hell mind, never the hell mind, for now. But don't think I'm not on to you."

I asked furiously, "Did you try and get me on the phone so you could hint around as much as you want to?"

"No, no. I sent some men to find you, but they said they couldn't, and what I wanted to know —"

"You wanted to check on the men and on me and probably on the answering service, too. You're the only guy I ever heard of who probably expects his shadow to hit him over the head one of these days."

"Listen, Savage, I've been trying to get you down to see me, and you can't blame me for wondering why you won't come here."

"Bull-oney!"

"Come down and see me before you do anything else. This is important."

"I still don't know what it's about."

"This needs the personal touch, Savage, face to face. I have to see you."

I didn't hesitate. Kowler might help me indirectly one way or another. Help was what I needed along with half a dozen arms and legs as well as eyes in the back of my head. And the trip wouldn't take long; I'd make sure of that.

"All right, I'll be there," I said.

"How soon?"

"That's me who just walked in."

The weak looking clerk behind the counter at the Ace Bookshop flipped a switch as soon as he saw me, and quickly backed up against the wall as if he was scared of my coming nearer. He didn't want to be contaminated. I'd have pinched his flabby cheeks playfully if he'd been any closer, but I wouldn't take one step to aggravate the likes of him.

The dark-painted door opened on Ziggy, who glared at me. His ugly face was white with venom. I guessed he'd have got a kick out of using the blackjack he carried in one hand. He'd never really be happy as long as I could stand up.

I weighed him with my eyes, taking in the small flat head and repulsively thick body tapering down to tiny girlish legs. The sight of him was enough to make anybody wince. He could hardly pass for a human being. He looked like something that had just crawled out from under a wet rock.

"What do they feed you on?" I asked softly. "What makes you think that the minute you've got a hunk of wood in your hand you're anything but a damn fool with a hunk of wood in your hand?"

"You'll find out fast enough." He stepped to one side, still looking squarely and unwaveringly at me. "In there, Savage, if you know what's good for you."

I did what he wanted, walking into the storeroom. The dust was a little thicker than last time, but nothing else had changed. Secondhand magazines were still roped into bundles against three walls. The display sign and life-size mannequin of a busty girl were set against the fourth wall, just as before. The dummy looked as permanent in this place as everything else did.

The office door was opened wide and Whit Kowler came charging out, walking with the angry tigerish movements I remembered having seen in him. Both hands were stretched tautly in front of him, almost like claws. His gray eyebrows were quirked in fury and he glared at me as if he were planning to grab for my jugular. Ten feet away from me he halted and stood growling.

"Where in hell is that movie?" he started finally.

"I don't know what you mean."

"You got that movie of Lore Wylie's out of Goodell's place and I want to know where it is." He pointed a crooking forefinger at my throat. "And I got a PS for you on that message: I'm *going* to find out, even if my boy here has to go kill you to do it. Is that clear?"

## FOURTEEN

"Nobody's going to kill me," I said thinly, "but I damn well want to know what you're talking about."

I glared at Kowler and quietly flexed my fists, forcing myself to keep my temper in leash.

"You're a double-crosser," Kowler snapped. "No more dependable than anybody else I ever met and you know it and I know it."

"Whether I'm a double-crosser or not, Kowler, I get mean when I don't know what people are talking to me about."

"Crap! You went to Goodell's apartment after we all left, right? That's a fact, isn't it?"

"It's probably in every newspaper in the whole country by now," I said easily. "Why in hell does it bother you so much?"

"You bought that movie from Goodell before he was killed. Damn it, I *know* you did."

"Goodell was as full of holes as a punchboard when I found him. The cops admit it. I couldn't have bought a damn thing from him."

"Then you found that movie there." Kowler leaned forward slowly. "I'm telling you I want it."

"For the last time all I ever found in Goodell's apartment was Goodell, and he was dead."

"Listen here, Savage, how many times do I have to tell you not to give me any crap? I've got no patience for this, you hear?"

"I want to know what makes you think I'm lying."

"All right, I'll tell you that. Christ knows why I'm so good to you, but I'll tell you that. I had Ziggy on your tail all the time, got that? You remember Ziggy now. He's looking right at you, just like I am."

"So Ziggy was on my tail, so what?"

"He says that when you left your apartment the next morning you purposely set out to break a tail. You did the old subway dodge and got away with it. What that means to me, Savage, is that you wanted to go someplace and peddle the movies for a higher price than I was offering. Well, you're not going to get away with that. The price is just what I told you last time and not a nickel more, and I'm the buyer. Get that straight once and for all."

I understood him now. He never would believe that I'd been out to get rid of the detectives who might be tailing me. He wouldn't believe anything but the worst. He was sure that there was a streak of bad in the best of us. That idea had made him a fortune. Nothing would ever convince Whit Kowler differently.

"You've got it wrong," I said, just to hear what my voice sounded like.

"Stupid bastard! Do you think I'm going to get shafted by you? It's been tried with experts, fella, and they fell flat every time. Give me that movie and you'll be all right."

"I haven't got —"

124

That was a sentence I didn't finish. Ziggy must
have come closer without my noticing it. A fist
landed unexpectedly against the right side of my
neck. I fell back, dazed. Stars whirled around this
place and the breath was crimped down inside me.
I managed to keep myself from falling and turned
around in what I hoped to hell was his direction.

It was. He charged me again, but I could make
him out and that changed the rules. I waited till I
could feel his breath fouling the top of the shirt I
wore, and then let go a right hook with everything
I had. It struck the point of his chin, doubling him
up backwards. He staggered and I began moving in
on him.

I didn't get far. Metal rapped the top of my
head, thumped the back of my neck and beat out
patterns against one temple and then the other. It
was Kowler using the barrel of a gun on me,
probably the Thunderbolt he carried.

Ziggy was back in the fight now. One of his fists
ripped my stomach in half and the other one caved
my chest in. I hit out blindly, making dents in the
air. Not a punch was pulled. The recoils and rolls,
the twists from side to side and arms flapping wide
were for real — and it's a lot more painful that
way, if anybody should ask about it. There was
nothing but a slim red rubber band of
consciousness in me and then there was a
gut-heaving wrench as the band snapped me into
deep darkness.

I was trying to climb a mountain by getting
holds on it with my nose, which felt as if it had
been rubbed raw. My whole body felt as if it had

been in a fire. After a deep breath I decided to open my eyes. The left lid wouldn't budge, and neither would the right. There was a pause before both eyes suddenly popped open and memories came flooding back to me.

I was on the dirty floor back of the Ace Bookshop, and bundles of magazines roosted against a foggy-gray wall some twelve feet away from me. Anybody who can find a wall can find a door and try to get his hands on whoever might be on the other side of that door.

Carefully I got up on my knees and plunked both palms down on the uneven floor that had bumps in it like hot cereal. Just as I anchored myself against the wall I heard a drawling voice: "That's real hard work you're doing."

Ziggy was grinning at me. Not even the stretched-out lips and the cheery glints in his slitted eyes made him look any less ugly as he watched me from his place in the middle of this storeroom.

"You think you're going anywhere?" he asked. "Don't put any dough on that."

As I took a deep, furious breath, baby-sounds came out of my throat.

"Not talking too good, huh?" His hatchet face glowed with obscene pleasure. "Whatever in the world happened to you, buddy?"

That made me so mad I found some of the words I wanted. "You repulsive goddamn hairy cockroach!"

Ziggy's chuckle died suddenly as he advanced on me. The fist I put up to defend myself hit out time and again with all the sturdiness of wet cardboard

126

flapping in a high wind. The hood kept himself away from my reach just the same, but swept his blackjack hard against the bridge of my nose.

A white-hot flame of anger kept me conscious as I dropped. I forced myself to lie face down on that floor while time cleared my head a little and sent some strength flowing back into me. My half-open eyes showed Ziggy returning to his previous place in the middle of this storeroom.

Too little time passed before I realized I couldn't make myself keep from another chance at that hoodlum bastard. Waiting patiently to get your hooks into a guy you hate isn't something that every human being can do.

I sat up and used both hands against the wall to help me stand as well as keep my balance. It may not have been easy, but I purposely made it look even harder by panting and swaying dizzily. That's an old trick I learned from a carny stunt man once: always look like you're under a strain after working in front of an audience or the rubes are sure to feel like they've been cheated.

Ziggy laughed. "Well, you got any more names you want to call me?"

"No," I said, forcing the word out. I swallowed noticeably. "Give me a butt."

"Why the hell should I give you anything? You called me a hairy cockroach."

"Forget that, will you?"

"You can't get no cigarettes out of cockroaches. They don't smoke."

"Look, Ziggy, I've been through the mill and I need a butt bad."

"So what am I supposed to do, jump up and

salute? When Kowler gets back from the business trip he's on, you'll really go through the mill. An emergency came up and sent him out for a while."

"Well, you could slip me one crummy butt, meantime."

Ziggy drew a cigarette out of a gold case and smiled when he deliberately threw it down on the floor at my side. He chuckled as I strained for it, grinning all over his ugly face when he heard me groan. He couldn't have had such a nice time since the night Lincoln died.

I popped one end of the cigarette into my mouth. "Got a match?"

He started to throw a gold lighter at me, but changed his mind. He didn't want the thing broken and I looked as if I'd have let it fall because I was so weak. As I swayed back and forth, he put the blackjack in a pocket where he could grab for it without much trouble, and came a couple of steps closer to me.

Long before the last possible split-second I took the only chance at him that I was likely to get, this time. I pulled my right hand up and put all the hate-made energy in me back of a punch. Bone and tooth were ground under my fist before Ziggy went over in a near somersault. His body hit the floor with a thud that was pleasurable to enemy ears. He lay still.

I glared down at him, then took one of the smut magazines out of a bundle and tore it into thin strips. After opening Ziggy's mouth I jammed the strips into it, then closed his mouth as much as I could. I saw his nostrils dilate as he breathed more vigorously through them, and wondered if I'd have

128

enough time to make the bastard eat that filth magazine page by page.

I decided that it would take too long to get such a petty revenge and looked up as if Kowler or the store clerk might be coming in at any time to raise an alarm and finish me off in this weakened condition.

Quietly I walked to the john and opened its small window. The day had grown darker, but I could make out a smooth square of sidewalk some ten or fifteen feet away. Easing myself out of the half-sized window wasn't any harder than opening it had been. I inched one foot out to the gritty stone ledge and then the other one. Once the lower half of me was out the window, I rolled over onto my belly and worked at getting the rest of me on that side of it. My shoulders are as wide as a stunt man's shoulders ought to be, so that I had to hunch them up a little in order to get through.

I jumped.

## FIFTEEN

At the nearest bathroom I checked on how much damage had been done. It looked like a lot. My face could have passed for a raw hot dog if not for the smudgy blackness around both eyes and a little swelling at the bridge of my nose. Both hands looked the same red color. But it wasn't really as bad as I'd been afraid it might be. Dirt had done my looks as much harm as anything else. That puffiness under the eyes would fade away in time, and so would the swelling on the bridge of my nose. A shower and change of clothing would make plenty of difference.

Rex wasn't fooled by the wash-up I'd taken, of course. It's almost impossible to hide anything like that from a dog. Knowing I'd had a rough time, she set up a howl and wouldn't let herself be calmed down till dinner.

The effect of a blue pin-stripe suit on me may not have made me look like a new man, but I didn't seem to have been roughed-up, either. I looked like nothing more startling than a tired businessman who could have legitimately run into a door. Strangers wouldn't gaze after me on the street. Little kids weren't likely to run away at the sight of me.

While the loin lamb chops were broiling a little later I made some phone calls. There'd been no news of Lore Wylie at Dutch County Hospital. The clerk at the hotel where she'd been staying hadn't heard from her, either. A reporter friend of mine, a fellow who works the morgue beat among others, told me that no tall young redhead had been sent there in the last day or so. Lore was still among the missing.

"Rexie," I told her as I served chopped liver, "something has to be done very fast and I haven't got a single idea."

The only idea in Rex's head was to shove food into herself. The sight of her gluttony didn't thrill me at all just then. The sound of it didn't do anything to me, either. Rex always ate with gusto.

My phone rang before I was finished with the chops, and I picked it up.

"Hello, passion flower, this is Jules Schlosser."

I pursed my lips disapprovingly. The big boss of Globe Studios probably wanted to know whether or not he ought to junk Lore Wylie's contract. He had asked me about it before, but the answer I'd given yesterday wouldn't satisfy him today. He'd be ready to ditch Lore without giving it a second thought.

"I asked you not to call me 'passion flower'," I said, more mildly than I'd thought I would.

"All right, sweetheart, don't get your ass in a sling. It's about our friend."

"Do you mean the girl I'm trying to help?"

"Sure, but I hate to have a name mentioned on the phone. Even hers."

"What do you mean, Jules, 'even hers'?"

"We've dropped her, lover, that's what I mean," he boomed. "She's off the contract list at Globe, and she isn't any concern of ours from now on. Whatever work you do for her won't cut any ice with the studio. I thought for sure that you'd want to know the financial picture has changed and you won't make much studio money out of this deal except a few bucks for the work you've done already. That's practically a debt of honor, sweetheart, so we're paying. But I figured that the least I could so was tell you about it."

"What made you drop her, Jules?"

"Because she's going to be in a lot of trouble before long, a first-class scandal and then some. It'll be a mess for her, and I don't want Globe pulled into any troubles of hers."

"She's carried a lot of Grade-Z stinkers for you people, carried them on her back and made winners out of 'em. You know that better than I do. A gesture of loyalty from you could mean a lot to her at this point in her life."

"I can't afford to get sentimental, lover. This isn't a hearts-and-flowers business."

"I still don't know why you suddenly decided to let her option drop, Jules. Did you get any new information about this since the last time you talked to me?"

"That I did, sweetheart," he said grimly, "but I'm not going to repeat it over the cross-country tube."

"Do you know where the girl is? Have you got any notion?"

"I can tell you exactly."

"Is she in Hollywood?"

"Yeh."

I had no idea why she'd gone home, but I knew what I'd better say to Jules. I made my voice urgent.

"All right, Jules, listen: I want you to do me and yourself and the girl a couple of favors. The first thing is to have a guard put on her, somebody who'll keep watch over her for every minute of the time."

"Well, look here, sweetheart, why should —"

"Quiet down and let me finish. The second thing I want you to do is to use your influence with some of those hot-shot New York business friends of yours to pull the local police off my tail so I can be dead sure they won't give me any trouble."

"I can't do that, Mark. Think it out, for God's sake! How can I stop a bunch of cops across the country if they want to do a certain job?"

"You know the answer to that, Jules. Most of the business you do is with bankers, and your people in New York can pass the word to a lot of higher-ups in the police department. The big cops have to listen when money talks, whether they like it or not. They'll pass the word down to lay off me. You know you can do it, Jules. I know it, too. Let's not talk fairy tales to each other. We're big boys now, and this is important."

"Not to me. The girl isn't with Globe any more. It doesn't really pay for the studio to get mixed up with it, if you know what I mean."

"Jules, did I ever steer you wrong?"

"No, I admit that. In fact, you did a whopping big job for me once, and God knows I'm still grateful." He was quiet for a full minute. "It won't be easy, but I'll do it."

"I knew I could depend on you."

"But wait a minute! What the hell am I doing it *for?*"

"To help me get out of town, Jules. I'm taking the first plane I can get back to your neck of the woods so I can talk to the girl."

"I think you've flipped for real this time," he told me. "There's no money in the job you're on, I keep telling you. No loot worth mentioning. You'll get paid off a few peanuts from the studio, like I said, but nothing more. Why do you want to knock yourself out on this?"

"Maybe I believe in an agreement once I've made it," I said shortly. "See you soon."

I made reservations with Pan Am for a jet that would be leaving in three hours. The prospect of a plane trip coast-to-coast was enough to make me irritable because I always hate to sit around for hours while my life is in somebody else's hands. If I'm going to be in any accident I'd want it to happen because I'm the one who goofed and not some pilot or mechanic or structural engineer. And if the work I did made any difference I wouldn't have to sit around as helpless as a baby should all hell break loose. In fact, I wouldn't have to sit around, period.

Short-tempered as I was, it took me longer than usual to make arrangements for handling Rex at the New York kennel where I generally leave her before going on a short trip from this section. I packed an overnight bag in my haphazard style and made arrangements with the hotel people to keep my room unoccupied for a day or so. After putting in a few miscellaneous phone calls I was ready to leave.

But it doesn't always pay to hurry. I got to Idlewild Airport with exactly thirty-one minutes to spare, and I paced the Pan Am building, hitting a fist against my palm till just before departure time.

## SIXTEEN

It was half-past ten on a warm, sunshine-spattered morning when the plane pulled in at Burbank's Union Air Terminal. It was a great day for swimming till noon and then putting in a little work with the golf clubs, all the time feeling sorry for those poor slobs in New York.

A cabbie drove me along the network of winding roads and into the city of small town customs and big town ideas. On the Boulevard, men in sports jackets and slacks walked the village-type promenade on their way to work in one of the skyscrapers. We passed the section between Sunset and Santa Monica, with its small hotels and taverns, bungalow courts and drive-in markets.

The cabbie, seeing me peering out from side to side, asked, "Your first time in sunny Cal, mister?"

"Believe it or not, I live in this town," I said. "The foothills."

"Oh." Respect tinged his voice. "You part of the industry?"

"I'm a stunt man, and that makes me part of the Screen Actors Guild," I said. "What made me buy a house I'll never know. If you're in the SAG these days, you're nothing but a migratory worker. Besides, peace and quiet don't appeal to me a hell of a lot."

"Move in around here." The cabbie pointed.

"You can get deaf at night from listening to the way cheap bedsprings creak up and down, up and down. Ah, what the hell! I've got a SAG card myself, but I got to drive a hack part time if I want to support a wife and three kids. I should'a become a stunt man myself, and then I'd be getting work a lot more often."

"Buddy," I said, watching him inch past a Fairlane that was swaying dangerously, "it looks to me like you're in the business whether you know it or — wait a minute! What are we hitting the strip for? Globe Studios isn't on Sunset and Gower where all the cheap-o outfits used to be."

"Is that where you want to go, mister, Globe Studios? When you got in the cab you gave me the name so quick I thought you said Gower and Sunset. Okay, mister, we'll go out to Culver City. That isn't too far away from here."

"Step on it, will you? . . .

Globe was a collection of butternut-colored buildings on Washington Boulevard only a few blocks past MGM. It couldn't have been anything else in the world but an entertainment factory, I saw, when a bored studio cop confirmed that I could go inside. Cowboys in make-up lounged around reading such trade papers as *Variety* and *Hollywood Reporter*. I passed a girl wearing the outfit of an Indian squaw and protecting some of her dyed black hair with a bright yellow handkerchief tied around her head. Extra players talked about "that movie we did with Rock Hudson," and I heard somebody saying thoughtfully, "All things considered, *Moby Dick* isn't a bad script."

Jules Schlosser's office was located in the building at the farthest end of the lot. Schlosser shook hands cordially after I had crossed the wide room to meet him. He smiled cheerfully, offered me cigars and asked if the deep cerise armchair I had taken was comfortable.

"Well," he said then, "how are things in little old New York? I envy you, moving around all the time. Wish to hell I could do it, sweetheart, and not see so much television all around me."

"You've done too many TV quickies, Jules."

"All we've done is to rent the facilities. Those goddamn actors outside are doing it. You didn't by any chance, think that Globe was still in the business of turning out quality movies for theatre exhibition, did you? That's just a sideline for us, these days. We're real diversified, we are."

He took a deep breath, which made him look even bigger than usual. He was good-sized anyhow, what with that heavy head and the thick hands, not to mention shoulders almost as wide as mine. He must have been in his mid-50's, and he had a bank account big as all outdoors. The money didn't keep him from worrying frantically about whatever might go wrong. He was a decent guy, considering the standard human product his business turned out.

"I don't know why the hell you want to have anything to do with Lore Wylie," he said suddenly, swivelling around in his chair to look through the big picture window. "When the balloon goes up, every paper in this country will have the straight scoop on her. Lore is all mixed up in the brainworks, you know that."

**138**

"I told her I'd help her and I'll finish it," I said to him. "Did you have a guard put on her? I asked you to take care of it for me."

"Hell, no! She's being guarded enough where she is. Lore don't need no more guards."

"Where is she?"

"At Maria Gomez', of course. Maria is practically with her all day and night. The two of them came back to town together from New York along with Lore's business manager, Harry Radfield. What makes Maria want to get mixed up in this is something I don't know, either. A friend's a friend, but what the hell! Lore is likely to knock herself off sooner or later."

"Where does Maria Gomez live?"

"Over at North Cliffwood Avenue in Brentwood Heights. She's got a guard who takes care of her, so look out. Things are a lot different for Maria than they were in Boston. When she was just plain Mary Gomer she didn't get far, but when she changed her name and picked up an accent she cracked the business."

"I guessed the accent was phony," I grinned reminiscently.

"Well, don't tell her I tipped you off." He looked puzzled when he added, "And I still don't know why you want to do so much for Lore Wylie. You're nothing but a social worker who happens to be a stunt man, that's all. There's hardly a dime in it, sweetheart. It doesn't make any sense to me."

"You know, Jules, what with one thing and another, I didn't think it would."

I went home briefly to get my black-and-tan

Peugeot from the garage, then stopped off at a drive-in barbecue stand. The meal was fair, and the accompanying scenery was downright fetching. A high-breasted blonde waitress in form-fitting slacks and a brass-buttoned jacket smiled and showed how nicely she could move while she hooked a silvery tray over the window of the Peugeot and nearly winked at me as she took my order. The impression I was meant to get was that I'd be sure to have a chance with her if I left a tip that was big enough.

Maria Gomez lived on a winding driveway lined with silk oak trees. A handball court, a tennis court and a swimming pool formed a triangle at the back and sides of the one-story white frame brick house.

I parked in an oval in front of the house and walked up to it. A man was already in the doorway waiting for me. He wore a male bikini the same color as the clear sky. It looked good on his muscular, tanned body or he wouldn't have worn it. His face was tanned, too, very smooth and unlined. His blonde hair might have been combed with glue, it was in place so firmly. He could have passed for a leading man in a cheap movie except that his eyes were too shifty.

"What's yours, bud?"

"I want to see Miss Gomez."

"She didn't tell me you were coming." The shifty eyes narrowed suspiciously.

"Was she supposed to tell you?"

"Miss Gomez always does."

"You're her appointments secretary, is that it?"

"Anybody she figures on seeing, she tells me to expect him."

"She'll talk to me. The name's Savage."

"Oh, so she'll talk to you, huh? Well, for your information, mister, I got orders that no visitors are allowed inside till further notice." He flexed his muscles, so that they seemed to be locked in an embrace. "Better dust out of here."

"Look, I've had a rough trip and I don't want —"

"I can call the cops if that'll make you feel better, wise man. Do you want me to?"

I grunted. In Brentwood the cops hate to see anybody who might just possibly twist a blade of grass sideways without having paid protection money first, let alone disturbing somebody who lived in one of the gold-plated houses.

"Make up your mind, wise man. I can take care of you personally if that'll make you happier."

"Remind me to pick up a flyswatter sometime and squash you."

It annoyed me to look defeated and to shrug helplessly and walk back to the Peugeot as if I was through. The muscle man's mocking laughter followed me part of the way.

A hundred feet down the drive, I stopped the car at one side, got out of it and walked back along grass that felt like lace underfoot. The silk oak trees hid me till I saw an open window at the left side of the house.

That window didn't give me any trouble. I found myself inside a big overfurnished living room done in tropical reds and vivid blue tones. It had been planned for a warm climate. I nearly expected to see mosquito netting on the windows and a pith helmet left on the spike back of the shepherd's chair or on the walnut planter that was bound with studded iron strips.

The silence was completely shattered by the noise of a fight. There would be a smack against flesh and an after effect, somebody letting out a breath. The spitting and snarling in between told me that both the fighters were women.

"Stay there, I tell you!" a voice commanded.

"No, you can't make me stay!"

The sounds were coming from behind a Seventeenth Century door with square-in-a-square carving set against the farthest end of this room. I ran to it, turned the knob swiftly and nearly fell into a bedroom done in wine red. After sizing up the situation I ran to Maria Gomez and forced her back and away from Lore Wylie. When Maria had moved back a few inches, I swiftly got between the two women.

Maria's dark dress had been ripped down the middle, and her heart-shaped face glowed after exertion. There was a faint trickle of what looked like red ink coming out of Lore's perfectly formed lower lip, and her deep red hair was mussed up. On the evidence, I'd have called their fight a draw. They had done enough damage to each other so that my getting between them could have passed for a good deed as far as they were concerned. Any urge to keep on with it drained out of both of them as I watched.

Lore sank down on the dark bedspread, dropped her head in her arms and began crying bitterly, hopelessly. There'd have been no stopping it, so I let her alone.

The door opened suddenly on the blond muscle

boy in the bikini. He took one glimpse of Lore and of Maria, then his eyes rested on me. He crouched grimly, made a pair of fists and started to move in my direction.

"You really asked for it, wise man," he said between clenched teeth. "Here's where you get it."

Maria told him sharply, "Don't, Raymond! There is no need."

Raymond hadn't been listening. He was too busy moving in on me slowly. He didn't have much idea of how wide-open he was. One feint and a punch deep in the gut would have finished him if I had tried the rush act. Fighting was a sport he had probably picked up in a girl's school.

Maria said sharply, "No, I tell you!"

Raymond hadn't heard that either. He was interested in the fight to come, nothing else. His shifty eyes were narrowed in concentration, his left fist already moving as if he'd punch me with it as soon as he got close.

Maria plunged out of my grasp and turned on him furiously. First she smacked him against one cheek, then the other. She followed that by drawing up a handful of his hair and half pushing, half kicking him to the door. She slapped him stingingly with every kick.

"Pig. Yellow-haired pig!" she stormed. "Yellow-haired pig, you! *Norteamericano* pig!"

Raymond didn't try to defend himself and maybe lose the things that counted in his life besides self-respect. He stood rigidly, a hand protecting both eyes while his face was slapped around and his legs kicked without mercy.

"Pig, yellow-haired pig! *Yanqui* pig! Out, out,

out of this room!"

He turned and ran from her. Maria slammed the door firmly and stood against it drawing deep breaths, the tilt of her breasts pushing in and out, thighs a little distance from the door and legs a few inches apart. I looked away quickly in order to keep control of myself.

Lore Wylie looked seductively dishevelled at the moment, too, her open pink bathrobe showing bright pink pajamas with a wide gash at the top. She covered it as I was turning toward her, drawing the lapels of her bathrobe closely together. Then she looked narrow-eyed at me as if she wanted to find out exactly how much of her skin I had managed to see.

"Why did you come out here, Mr. Savage?" she asked finally. "Not just to peep, I'm sure."

"One reason is that I wanted you to know I figure to wrap up your troubles in a very little while. What I promised I'd do is still straight goods as far as I'm concerned."

"I thought I told you — look here, *can* you do anything to help? The most important thing is to get hold of that vile movie or prove it was made by a double for me."

"I'm doing my damnedest, Lore. You always think I'm out leching or whatever, but I've worked this case day and night so I can get rid of it fast and go back to stunting again."

"That movie will finish me if it's ever seen," she said. "Nothing else is going to hurt me as much."

"What else is there?" I put in. "You've been making hints about something else, and I've got a perfect right to know what. I'm working hard for

144

you and if I don't get full cooperation from you now it can take God knows how much longer to handle this."

Lore shrugged. "If I could tell you about the movie I'm sure I can tell you about this."

Maria put in warningly, "Shut up, *chiquita!*"

"No, Maria. As far as I'm concerned, the scandal about that sex movie is the most terrible thing that can happen to me. Anything else can't be so bad, even though the law says it's much worse."

"*Chiquita*, it would be a mistake to tell about what I am sure is on your mind."

"What I did doesn't involve anything dirty." She faced me again. "I killed a man on account of that hellish movie. I stabbed him to death."

The sudden quiet in this room was starting to crawl up my nerve-ends and twist them viciously. I worked my irritation off by whirling around on Maria and snapping:

"Have you got any liquor in this dump?"

Maria opened the door and shouted, "Drink! *La bebida!*" She left the door open. Her combination butler, lover, bodyguard and punching bag came hustling into the living room and quickly opened a liquor cabinet above the television set in the farthest corner. He made one drink, then set it down deftly on a tray and waited.

"Order me a gin-and," I told Maria. "Your buddy will feel better if I don't talk to him."

Maria passed the order along. The muscle boy built my drink and carried it in on a tray along with a whiskey sour for Maria. Lore, I guessed, was an abstainer. The gin-and soaked into me. I didn't say a word till I had finished it and the bikini boy had done another vanishing act.

"Tell me what happened, Lore," I suggested finally. "All of it."

"His name was Goodell, Robert Goodell," she started, very quiet. "I knew him because he photographed one of my first movies. We used to argue about camera angles. He insisted on making me look like a — a prostitute, a streetwalker. Well, that doesn't make any difference. The point is that I knew his voice right away when he phoned me at the hospital."

"What did he say?" I prodded after she'd been pausing too long. "Tell me what he wanted."

"Goodell started by saying that he hoped I was all right and that he had recently sent me a very special photograph, and he hoped I'd be interested in it because it was part of a movie that might become very well known. Then he said he wanted to see me as soon as possible in his apartment in Greenwich Village, and he gave me the address."

"So you went?"

"Of course," she said in quiet shame. "It was the first time I ever wanted to go to a man's apartment and be alone with him, but there wasn't any help for that."

"Why in hell didn't you call me?"

"Because you were out of it as far as I was concerned. How could I have know that you'd want to make an impression on me by staying with the case?"

"I didn't — all right, all right. Tell me the rest of it."

"I was able to get away from Dutch County

Hospital without any trouble, thanks to Maria. I went straight to Goodell's apartment as if I was his — his mistress or something like that."

"Never mind the moralizing. Tell me how your talk with him came off."

"He was walking around in a very woozy kind of a way when I got there. I thought he was drunk but he said he'd been given a hard time a little while ago by some crooks and that he'd be good as new in no time."

"Get to the point, Lore. What else did he tell you?"

"He said he'd convince me of what he had nerve enough to call the truth, that I had made the movie. If I paid him to suppress it, he said, he'd earn as much money from me as from any filth peddler in town. I told him I'd want to see that unholy movie and find out just how well it had been faked."

"Did Goodell cooperate?"

"He nodded at the start and said that what I was asking for was only fair and that I certainly had every right in the world to see the movie. Then he asked me if I'd like to make myself comfortable and have a drink or have something to eat."

"And I suppose you told him to stick to business. Then what?"

"He suddenly started to stare at me. It was a complete surprise. He might have been weighing me on a scale or judging me. I couldn't think why, except that I'd been very excited and when a woman looks that way a man becomes stimulated — uh, sexually." She flushed at what she'd just said. "Then Goodell gave a hideous leer and told me that he'd always thought I wasn't really cold or frigid, but that I was a hot little piece giving a good time to most of the men on the Globe lot."

"In other words, Goodell was making a condition before he'd even talk to you about selling the movie."

"That's what it came down to. I was stunned and very quiet at first. I'd been desperate to get any information to help me find out about that movie. I didn't say a word to Goodell, but I remember thinking that if only I could give him what he wanted very, very quickly without a word between us, then I might go along with it."

"But I suppose that wasn't his idea," I prodded her again. She'd have lapsed into a dazed quiet, otherwise. Already she seemed to have been paralyzed from the head down and she gazed unseeingly around her.

"He started to say how much he liked me and what we'd do together in bed — terrible things, obscene things that I never heard before from a human being. And then he put an arm around me and brought up his other arm to one of my breasts and squeezed hard. That was all I could stand. I realized what was happening. When he brought his right arm around towards me, I moved away from him. He blocked me. It happened very fast, like in a movie. He stood in front of me and came at me. We were in the living room. There was a fruit knife on the table. I grabbed it up — it was the first thing I'd touched with my hands since the trouble happened. I plunged the knife into him.'

She didn't seem stunned now. The memory of a

148

killing done in self-defense was something that she could take in stride. Only the thought of a man's overtures got her upset, twisting her values even further out of all recognition.

"What happened after you stuck a fruit knife into Goodell?"

"I pulled it out because I'd been holding on to it so tightly all the time that it came away with me. Goodell blinked and drew a deep breath, but that was the only reaction he showed. I guess he was so absorbed in what he was doing — like any man would be, I'm sure! — that he didn't realize what had happened."

"And he kept coming after you?"

"Yes, that's right. I got into a frenzy and used the knife on him again. This time he fell back, but not for long. I ran out to the foyer but he followed and put a fat greasy arm around me. As soon as he touched me I turned and stabbed him a third time and when he fell back the point of the knife was inside him, so I left it and ran."

"Did anybody notice you going in or out of the apartment?"

"No. I'd have seen the leering looks, believe me, but there wasn't one person in the hallway either when I came in or when I left."

"And then I suppose Maria made arrangements for you to fly home with her," I said resignedly, feeling empty and a little dead, myself. "Did you wear gloves all the time you were there?"

"Yes. I wouldn't take them off while I was in that apartment alone with him, or relax in any way."

"There's a chance, then, that the cops might

never know you were mixed up in what happened. If I can make sure of that and make sure the stag movie is destroyed and do it all in a day or so it'll be the damnedest piece of work I ever pulled off."

"Yes, and I suppose I could pick up my career after that," she said. "There won't be any sex scandal and I'll be able to get a job at one of the other studios or with an independent producer."

"How come Globe dropped your contract, by the way? I forgot to ask Jules."

"The official reason is that I was asked to play the part of Sadie Thompson in Globe's remake of *Rain*, and I turned it down. It's true, of course, but the only reason I was asked to do something that everybody knew I wouldn't do was to give Globe a reason to drop me."

"What's the actual reason they let you go?"

"Schlosser was told that I once made a 'stag' movie, and that the story couldn't be hushed up. When he said it over the phone, there was such an I-told-you-so leer in his voice I thought I'd collapse from shame — and I'd never actually done anything."

"Who gave Schlosser the story?"

"My business manager, that's who. Correction: my *ex*-business manager. Harry Radfield decided I wouldn't ever be a money-maker again and took his story to Globe so he could get on Jules Schlosser's good side. He knows that Jules appreciates favors but he doesn't realize that Jules hates a double-crosser."

"Radfield makes plenty of bloopers," I said, remembering the monocled, pseudo-efficient guy who did so many things wrong. "He and a few other bums in this town are going to be sorry for the raw deal they've handed you."

"Can you do something to make sure, *chico?*" Maria Gomez's eager hot brown eyes searched my face with every forward step she took, and she swayed gently as if carrying a basket on her head. "Well, *chico?* Tell me now if you can do something."

"I told the two of you before that I'll try my damnedest. Do I have to repeat that every minute?"

"But can you make sure what you do will be effective?"

"I'm not going to do anything I know will be useless, baby. You can bet money on that."

"But is this not — how you say? — obstructing the justice?"

I grinned at the recollection of hearing about her having been born in the exotic town of Boston. "It won't bother me a lot, morally. I don't think anybody who knew much about Goodell could really care if his killer gets away with it. Goodell wasn't much of a loss and the killing was obviously done in self-defense. It's hard to feel that he had a tough break."

Maria accepted that with a nod. "And you say you can find out about the filthy movie?"

"Right."

"This would make the difference to Lore." She smiled at me. "One other thing, *chico:* you owe me the apology for what you did to me the last time we saw each other."

"For slapping your face, you mean?" I had almost forgotten our New York City cab ride together after I had sais something about her accent. "What makes you bring that up, now?"

"Call it," Maria's smile was like slow music, and you could almost hear castanets clicking languidly not too far away, "an investment in friendship. Any woman likes to have some good friends, if you know exactly what I mean."

"I know, and I appreciate what you're saying." It took an effort to recall how she had been at my throat the last time I'd seen her. An imagined insult, a non-existent slight, could make her revert to a vicious animal. "Believe it or not, though, my temper is nearly as bad as yours is."

"I don't have the really bad temper, *chico*, because I forget after a while whatever it was that made me angry."

"While you're angry, though, you're a pretty hard customer, Maria," I grinned. "Besides, I could never know in advance what'd get you sore. It's like handling a bomb when you haven't got any notion what makes it active."

Maria Gomez didn't become irritated, as I'd have figured. Instead she seemed to draw back inside herself, to shrink a little as I watched. A red streak flushed her tawny skin and she looked away.

Lore Wylie threw a keen glance at Maria, but now she turned, cleared her throat awkwardly, rubbed her palms against the bathrobe she wore, straightened up nervously and faced me with a hesitant smile stretching her lips.

"Mr. Savage, can I tell you something?"

"If you want to."

"It's a story that Maria knows already, but she'll probably excuse me for repeating. It's about a little girl whose parents were very firm with her on one point. They taught her never to doubt that men and boys from sixteen onwards wanted only one thing from a girl. The evil ulterior motives of all men made them untrustworthy, these parents said. No man wants to get married if he can get something 'bad' in a different way. Do you understand this, Mr. Savage?"

"So far, so good. What's the rest of it?"

"The parents were fine people otherwise — let me make that point clear before I go any further. They were honest, respectable and God-fearing. The father had made a lot of money without losing the religious feeling he'd always had. The mother was religious, too, and she was a wonderful woman in every way except the one I mentioned before."

"She was as hipped on sex as her husband was," I said, nodding. "What happened to the little girl?"

"When she grew older she said that she wanted to be a movie actress. The parents disapproved bitterly. They said that Hollywood was an immoral town. They showed her news stories about Hollywood scandals and divorces and loose living. The parents had been raised at a time when the town used to spawn scandals. But they finally decided not to stand in the way of the girl's finding herself. As I said, they were good people."

"They twisted their daughter's life around, it seems to me."

"But they didn't know they were doing any harm," Lore said. "They wouldn't have hurt their child knowingly for any money in the world."

"I don't think any parents would," I said pleasantly, "but a lot of them do."

"Let's not talk about that right now, if you don't mind," Lore suggested. "The girl I was telling you about, Mr. Savage, became a success in this town. She had prestige and she had money. Socially, though, she was a washout."

"That isn't what I'd call a surprise."

"No, I guess not. Men kept away from her, never tried to do anything for her unless it was important for them. Why go out of the way otherwise? They knew they wouldn't even get a thank-you because the girl was always very suspicious."

"She can't have got much of a boot out of living," I said slowly. "It wouldn't surprise me if a girl like that tried to kill herself when something went seriously wrong in her life."

"Eventually she met one man who wouldn't take her usual attitude as final," Lore Wylie said. "This man insisted he had made up his mind to help her and he'd do it no matter how much trouble she gave him. A good man, a decent man. A man who wasn't selfish, and didn't seem to have any evil ulterior motives... well, the girl was grateful and wanted to say so, to thank a man from the bottom of her heart for the first time, and to mean it sincerely."

"If she did, it would be appreciated," I said, keeping very calm. I didn't want her becoming all emotional, so I added in a businesslike way, "I'll report to you in person on what happens. But I hope you won't try to escape from anything at all till you hear from me again."

"I promise I won't," she said awkwardly, "if you tell me that there's a chance it'll be all right for me."

154

Maria Gomez glared from me to Lore and back again, her mouth thinly disapproving, her hot brown eyes narrowed to angry slits as if she'd have liked to string up the two of us from the nearest pole. For some reason I didn't know, she'd be in a hating mood till the pendulum swung back the other way and then she'd wonder how Lore could ever think of her as anything but a constant friend.

"There's a chance," I told Lore.

And Maria, that implacable foe, now gave me an encouraging smile before raising her eyes and saying devoutly:

"God willing."

## SEVENTEEN

It was half-past six in the evening when I groped my way out of the jet at Idlewild. Twenty-four hours hadn't passed since I'd been across the country and back. For once I was a little tired.

I got in touch with Whit Kowler at the Ace Bookshop a few minutes after finding a telephone. "I'm coming over to see you."

"I won't be here," Kowler said, automatically suspicious. "What makes you want to see me?"

"To talk business."

"You expect me to believe that all of a sudden you want to talk business with me?"

"Believe what you want to, but I'm going to drop in on you just the same."

"No, hold it. Goddamn, I'll pick a place where I can make sure you don't bring ten million cops with you. Be in the Hotel Howat over on Thirty-fourth and First at eight o'clock exactly. If I'm satisfied there's nobody with you, we'll talk."

I hung up first. Back in the hotel room I drew out a nickel-plated Smith & Wesson .38 from my overnight bag and, holding it by the stag grip, checked the swing-out cylinder to make sure every one of the six chambers was carrying its load of ammo. I dropped it into a leather spring-holster and belted it on. The gun might help in getting rid

156

of Kowler and Ziggy once and for all. On account of Lore Wylie alone, it had become necessary.

I got to the appointment early. Kowler came stalking into the dim, high-ceilinged lobby at exactly ten minutes past the right time. He moved across the deep pile rug swinging his large head from left to right. After nodding warily at the sight of me, his eyes narrowed at the people on my right and left. He gave a satisfied nod after a minute of that, and came close.

"Well, Savage? Are you going to try and pull a fast one about the movie you took from Goodell?"

"I didn't take anything from Goodell. What I want is to talk to you in some place that's quiet."

"What are you up to? You can't louse me up like you did with Ziggy, stuffing that magazine in his mouth. I'm not — the hell!"

Kowler suddenly jumped up when his left shoulder was grasped by a thin white hand, but gave an easy smile when he saw who had done it.

"Oh, it's you," he said pleasantly. "A little early for the appointment, aren't you?"

"Only a few minutes." The newcomer smiled vacantly. He was a middle-aged man with an oddly blank face that belonged in an amateur's drawing. Yellow had been filled in clumsily for color, the nose looked broken and the glazed dark eyes couldn't ever have been pleased by anything. Two white wings at the top of his head were supposed to be hair. "Is this gentleman a friend of yours?"

"We know each other," Kowler admitted, adding ungraciously, "Savage, McGovern."

McGovern offered a flabby hand that lingered a shade too long in mine.

"Why doesn't he join us?" McGovern asked Kowler. "I think it would be a fine idea."

"Savage is pretty busy and I didn't figure on —"

"Well, I'd like to have somebody else's opinion of the merchandise Kowler has got," McGovern said, aiming that vacant smile at me. "Can you spare us a few minutes?"

It wasn't hard to imagine what sort of merchandise Kowler was peddling. If it *had* been hard, a glance down at the large leather portfolio under his right arm would have tipped me off for sure. The portfolio looked bulky enough to hold at least one can of film. Although I could have easily got along without another whiff of pornography, I didn't want to lose track of Kowler. It might have taken me too much time to get hold of him again. The sooner my business with him was settled up, the better I'd like it. That was the number one reason for my coming back to this city now.

"Thanks," I said to McGovern. "I'd be glad to help."

"That's fine," he told me, nodding. "Please come with me, gentlemen."

He led the way to a large comfortable elevator and out of it to the plushy suite of rooms he lived in. An expensive movie projector was set up at the far end of the tastefully decorated living room, and a movie screen had been put against the nearest wall, practically hiding a painting that didn't look to me like a reproduction. McGovern was obviously a man who would have been able to afford any vices he took to.

"This is a brand-new film, Mr. McGovern," Kowler said agreeably, taking it out of the

158

portfolio and putting it on the projector. "Just been brought in from *la belle France.*"

"Don't try to fool me," McGovern said. "It's probably a print of a movie that isn't useful to you any more, so you're unloading it on me because I'm a collector."

"I wouldn't lie to you about a thing like that, Mr. McGovern," Kowler said, almost as if he were sincere. "Besides, the picture is a lot of fun, and that's something that never yet did any harm to a man's glands."

"Depends on the man's age and condition."

Kowler chortled hollowly. He had probably made his last remark on purpose, expecting to hear a mild joke that would let the prospect put himself in a better frame of mind. Kowler needed to be a first-class salesman, of course, but I hadn't realized how good he was. He'd most likely have been able to sell Brooklyn Bridge to the Mayor of New York.

The run-off started on a movie called *The Whipping Post.* But it hadn't been on for more than ten or fifteen seconds when Kowler put a thick hand against the cam in order to freeze the movement.

"Keep it going," McGovern said urgently.

"Sure I will, Mr. McGovern. It gets so hot later on that it's worth every cent of five hundred dollars."

"That's too much. I never paid five hundred dollars for a movie before."

"Well, I'm sorry, if we can't do business —"

"I'd like to look at the movie, though. Please."

"Afraid that can't be done on a browsing basis, Mr. McGovern. It was brought into this country at considerable expense and it's in excellent condition. If there was a rip in it anywhere, I'd have to sell it for less to the collector who did buy it."

"Wouldn't a hundred and fifty be all right for it? Five hundred seems like so much money to pay for something like that."

"I'm sorry, but I can't possibly give it away for a dollar less than five hundred. I'd like to, but you know the kind of risks a man has to run in this business."

"It's robbery. You ought to be put in prison and the keys thrown away."

"If I could keep my risks down, Mr. McGovern, I'd be able to charge lower prices. This way, I'm afraid I can't oblige."

"All right, all right, let the thing run. I can afford to pay a little extra for it."

McGovern wrote a check very slowly when the movie was done. Finally he tore it out of the book and set it down inch by inch at the other end of his desk. He raised an arm to gesture Kowler out of the place, and that arm was still in mid-air when the two of us left. He hadn't looked at me since I had walked in here. My advice would not have been what he'd wanted even if he had asked for it.

Kowler examined the check thoroughly before he put it away in a zippered wallet which he tucked into a breast pocket and then tapped a couple of times.

"You must be selling him duplicates that can't make you any more money." I said, feeling a little sick to my stomach. "And probably sending the originals overseas."

"The old stupe don't care about that." Kowler's face twisted with the usual contempt of the panderer for his customers, the ones on the other side of the same greasy coin. "Perverts, animals, every single one of 'em."

Kowler suddenly dug me in the ribs, and I looked aside to see him glancing down at the .38-size bulge under my left arm.

"I want the hardware you're carrying, Savage." His voice was sharpened to a note of angry command as he jabbed metal against my ribs a second time. "Open your jacket and give it to me very slow, business end first. I wouldn't mind knocking you off right here and now if you don't play ball. If I'd seen it before, I would've clobbered you for sure. Give!"

I did it, except for giving him the gun quickly. I almost threw it into his free hand.

"Now we'll go to my office and find out what's really itching you. Maybe me and Ziggy can fix you up between us."

Kowler drove the Cad and watched me most of the time he was doing it, the .22 in one hand so that he'd be able to use it promptly if I acted up. I sat quietly at the other end of the front seat, trying to keep myself from a stunt that involved working against an amateur who was liable to kill the two of us. Long experience told me that there's no percentage trying anything rask in a car unless I'm at the wheel, myself. I remembered seeing the wreckage of a car and two men who had been co-workers of mine. They had belonged to the Black Cat Club, too, whose thirteen members did their most dangerous stunts on Friday the thirteenth; but a dry run in a car was the last work they ever did. Luckily I didn't have to sit in Kowler's car and control myself too long before we got to the closed front of the Ace Bookshop.

Kowler looked up and down the street and then fumbled with the front door lock, promptly snapped down the burglar alarm inside as well as flicking on one of the fluorescents. Then he gestured me inside. After making sure that nobody could look in, he locked the door from this side.

When we got to his office, he checked his distance from me and got on the phone to Ziggy. "Hop over here and bring your tools. I've got a guest you'll want to see for sure."

"You mean Sav — . . .?"

"No names on the phone, stupid! How many times do I have to say you never know who's listening?"

"All right, all right." Ziggy chuckled. "Don't make any dents in my pal till I get there."

I waited till Kowler had hung up and said, "You and Ziggy won't get to lay a glove on me this time, let alone 'tools' like blackjacks or brass knucks."

"What does that mean?"

"Just this, Kowler: the main reason I wanted to see you was to tell you a certain fact in person. I've been looking forward to this since I got on the plane at Burbank."

"Where's the catch?" Suspicion-lines appeared at the corners of his thick lips. "There's gotta be something or you wouldn't be so happy."

"Uh-huh," I said, "and I'll give it to you short and sweet. You're hung up by the nose, Kowler.

162

That movie isn't worth any more or less to you than the average stag movie you deal in."

"What the hell are you yapping about?"

"The movie won't bring in extra money no matter how fast you get it or how little it costs." I gestured irritably. "How many times do I have to say something in English?"

"You expect me to believe this song-and-dance?"

"Sure I do, and I'll tell you why I expect you to go along with what I'm saying. I've been finding out about Lore Wylie by talking to her, and you can get the same information a lot quicker by asking anybody else who knows her if I'm lying about what I'll tell you right now. Lore Wy — ..."

"Any information I want I'll get at first-hand without asking for it."

"Okay. You arrange to meet her and spend a little time with her and then make up your own mind if she could possibly have made a movie of that kind."

"Hell, you can't expect her to admit it! She must'a done the hot pic when she was younger and she needed eating money."

"Another woman might've, sure, but not Lore Wylie. There isn't a man who's talked to her and who wouldn't go along with that; I'd bet on it. Maybe she isn't frigid or even close to it, but she definitely wouldn't have any part of a deal like this."

"So what? Goodell might'a used some broad who looked like her in that movie he photographed. The perverts who watch those damn movies, they wouldn't know any difference."

"Sure they would. Even in a crummy movie like one of those, you can't fool an audience that way. Don't forget you're dealing with close shots and the audience pays a lot of attention to magnified photographs of faces. It's impossible to use a substitute actress in such close work. That's something I know about, Kowler. It's a subject I've had to look into in my time. I couldn't be fooled about any kind of stunting whatsoever or what has to be done in order to make it successful."

"The broad herself is behaving like the story is true, from what I hear. She tried to kill herself yesterday or the day before, whenever it was."

"You were just telling me you don't believe what you hear from other people," I reminded him. "What makes you go along with this story?"

"I'm not going along with it," Kowler snapped. "It's a rumor and I repeated it, that's all."

Kowler stood up, warily moving the hand with the gun that could rip into a kneecap or heart. He looked me up and down as the whole truth was printed on me somewhere.

"Goodell offered me that movie and I'd bought half a dozen other ones from him," Kowler said. "I told Ziggy what Goodell claimed he had, and Ziggy passed the word to plenty of good customers like Charlie Osterman. The trouble with Ziggy is that he believed it absolutely — either that, or he wanted to put me on a spot. But I figured from the start that Goodell might be lying to get some extra money for himself."

"Do you mean to tell me you never believed him?"

"I wasn't sure one way or the other and I'm still

not." Kowler's teeth flashed between thinned lips. "I won't know for sure till I see the picture, so I'm going to keep hunting till I do, and there isn't anything you can say that'll stop me."

"For God's sake!" It made me angry for the moment to know beyond question that the showdown between us would have to be studded with violence. "I'm giving you the only possible answer and you think I dreamed it up. How stupid can a human being possibly get?"

"He can't get so stupid he'll take somebody's word when it comes to making dough. You come in here and try to sell me a story and you figure I'll swallow it because you say I ought to. That's a crock of baloney, and you know it as well as — what in hell is keeping Ziggy? He probably stopped off for a couple of minutes with one of his goddamn two dollar broads, the double-crossing bastard!"

I was watching Kowler when he turned irritably and lifted part of the shade over the doorway. His back grew rigid with anger. Suddenly he let the window shade pop up and whirled around on me.

"Look at that, goddammit! Look!"

A black car was being parked across the street near the lamppost. Blue-uniformed men with guns held steady got out of it. The last man out was wearing plainclothes. His heavy appearance told me that it was Lieutenant Jessup, the big slow-moving patient guy who had talked to me not long ago. He held out a warning hand before one of his underlings, then turned and started walking to this block.

He rapped on the door.

Kowler had put his gun away, but now he hesitated. He didn't open the door till Jessup's rapping had become more persistent, and then he held it less than six inches open so that he could slam it shut at any time.

"What do you want?" Kowler demanded.

"To get inside."

"You need a warrant."

"My potsy here says that I don't," Jessup rumbled in the deep voice I remembered. "If this wasn't a public street, buster, and I didn't have some respect for citizens, you'd get smacked around like you goddamn well deserve."

"This is a legitimate business I'm running here. You've got no right to come bothering me. I'm going to call my lawyer."

"And while you're doing it, I may have the door battered down," Jessup snapped. In this light, he looked big enough to do the job himself. "That makes it a Mexican standoff, except that you lose."

"All right, all right," Kowler muttered. "Just you, though, mister. Nobody else comes in here."

"We'll see."

Kowler didn't have any choice but to give in. He stepped to one side. Jessup was already scowling before he clumped inside, and nothing changed in his expression when he saw the magazines taped at the outside center and the books wrapped in cellophane. His lips were pursed disapprovingly, as if something that smelled had been put in front of him.

"The beat cops must be making a pile of dough from this operation," Jessup said grimly. "And the

166

vice squad boys, too. There must be plenty of gravy for the local lads in a deal like this."

"I'm not saying a thing unless there's a lawyer here," Kowler told him.

"I'd like to take your customer lists and check them against any known sex perverts — as if I didn't know what I'd find. In fact, I might do it just to be aggravating."

"Without a warrant?"

"Sue me after I've done the damage."

"You think you can break the law any time you want, just because you're a cop." Kowler's attitude changed almost before he had finished saying that. He cleared his throat, forced a smile, rubbed both hands together and managed to look friendly. "See here, you sounded a little jealous of the vice squad boys just before, but they don't have to be the only ones making a few bucks. I'm pretty sure you and me can do business."

"This ought to be good." Nothing changed on Jessup's flabby face. "What's your offer?"

"Just to get out of the nuisance of having my files taken away is worth, oh, a G note."

"I'd figure it was good for at least tne of them," Jessup said surprisingly.

"I can't afford that many."

"Well, five G's wouldn't be selling myself down the river for peanuts, either. I'd settle for that."

"You're driving a hard bargan, but I think I could manage two thousand."

"And the men?" Jessup pointed a fat thumb towards the door. "They'd have to be taken care of."

"A hundred apiece extra ought to do it for

them."

Jessup turned and lifted one hand. It must have been a signal. The door opened on a uniformed cop who came in hesitantly. Three other men joined him. All of them stood shoulder-to-shoulder, waiting to hear what Jessup wanted.

"What do you think just happened, boys?" he started. "I was offered a bribe."

Kowler tried to say something, but bit it off after one look from the fat lieutenant.

"Me, I like money and I've always envied the people who get it. This offer is for two grand. On top of that, each of you boys gets a hundred apiece. Do you boys think we ought to take it?"

One of the younger cops said promptly, "Not if it means easing up on a bastard like this."

"I'll go along with you, Donovan," Jessup said pleasantly. "I suppose the rest of you feel the same way. Right? . . . Good. You can wait in the car."

The men left silently. We didn't hear the door closing. Their footsteps outside were like muted metronomes. Nobody could have called them clumsy.

"I just wanted to show you that there are a few cops left who don't like to grab dirty money." Jessup said. "Now, do you want to find out why I came here? Do you really want to get down to business now?"

## EIGHTEEN

"All right, you made your point." Kowler stood with narrowed eyes, hands tight against his sides. "Why did you come here? What do you want?"

"To find out who killed Robert Goodell," Jessup said quickly. "I'm a homicide man and that's my job."

"Where do I come into it?"

"I've looked up Goodell, and I know he used to be a Hollywood cameraman, but he wasn't able to get work there. He raised money by making and selling hot movies in this city. I didn't know who his outlet was. But now I do."

"You're guessing."

"Not any more." Jessup seemed to look my way for the first time. "You led one of my men down here, which is something you might be glad about; I'm not sure. You weren't altogether as smart as you figured. Some of your influential friends told my bosses to keep off your track for a while, so we did that. But we got in touch with the airline people and the California police, you see. As soon as you booked passage back from Burbank, I was told about it, and I sent one of my men out to the airport to pick up the trail. He's been on to you ever since then." Jessup turned back. "Well, buster?"

"You haven't proved anything yet." Kowler paced up and down the store, pausing to straighten out a magazine display that showed a man in a G-string lifting a barbell. "All you've done is talk."

"Now that I've found a possible outlet — we'll put it that way, Kowler — I won't have any trouble getting hold of people you've dealt with, and who can prove you did business with Goodell."

"I *met* Goodell," Kowler said sullenly. "At a party once, I met him. That's all."

Jessup looked at me again. "You got anything you want to say, Savage?"

Jessup's cautiously expectant look in my direction tipped me off that he was expecting to play me against Kowler and maybe get a frenzied accusation that could help him crack the murder wide open. I smiled grimly at this unexpected meshing of his careful plans and my hurriedly made ones; nothing would have made me happier than for Robert Goodell's murder to be pinned on Kowler or Ziggy or both of them.

"I'm willing to tell you whatever I know," I said. "Your M.E. probably gave you the information that Goodell had taken a beating the day he died — right?"

"What about it?"

"He was handed that beating by Kowler and by a hood who works for him, a hood called Ziggy."

I left out almost as much as I rattled off, telling Jessup what had happened the first time I'd been in Goodell's apartment. Lore Wylie's name didn't come into my account at all, nor did any details of what I'd wanted from Goodell, or that I'd come back to this place with Kowler and Ziggy

**170**

afterwards because of the .22 that Kowler probably carried all the time. Otherwise I told it straight, and quickly.

Kowler listened with intentness, his body crouched and his hands like claws as if he were going to spring at me the minute I said something that wasn't true.

"Listen to me, Kowler," I said to him, raising my voice. "There isn't any way of knowing that Ziggy didn't go back and work Goodell over again that night. If Ziggy did it on his own, you can't be responsible for anything he might have done while he was there."

"What are you getting at?" Kowler asked fiercely. "What are you trying to prove?"

"That Ziggy isn't any more loyal than the other people who work for you," I suggested, still keeping my voice loud. "Ziggy could see a chance to get hold of some valuable merchandise and charge the boss extra money for it, so he's as likely to do it as anybody else is."

"Yeh, and you're as likely to slip me another double-cross, too. I want to talk to a lawyer."

"There's no time for that," I said swiftly.

"I'll find time."

"You'll be without a business if you do," I snapped. "Jessup will keep working the way he'd figured on up to now. He'll rip your business to pieces. Since what you're doing is mostly illegal anyhow, you'll be ruined even if you don't get sent to prison. Either you lose your business or you give us the testimony that'll help send Ziggy away for a long time, maybe forever."

"But then I'd be prosecuted, too."

"No, Kowler, the Lieutenant will see to it that you'll be immune from prosecution if you testify against Ziggy in a court. That's the best deal you can make, and you'd better make it before whatever patience I've still got is exhausted and I go to work on you, personally."

"It's probably the best deal at that." Kowler threw his shoulders back. "What the hell, Ziggy's no better than the restof 'em. He probably figured he could buy the picture from Goodell or scare it out of him, and he went back to try. As a matter of *fact*, I asked him to go back and not to use any violence at all. The next time I saw Ziggy and asked him if Goodell had changed his mind, Zig smirked and said that I'd never have any trouble with Goodell again. I could hardly trust that ugly bastard anyhow, and he must'a crossed me someti — . . ."

"This ugly bastard never went against you, boss," Ziggy said thinly. "Till now."

He opened the inside door as he talked, having got into this place by its back entrance. His spindly legs swayed under the weight of that large grotesque body. The thin cruel face was twisted by anger. His right hand was bent around the lower part of a blackjack, and the wood looked natural there; it was an appendage to Ziggy's body, the symbol of his power.

"Good thing I came over, huh, boss? Good thing you told me to come, huh? That we'd have a fine time taking Savage apart. Right, boss?"

"Look, Ziggy, you don't understa — . . ."

"I heard it. I'm just an ugly bastard, but I got

ears. It's me or you, so you're throwing an ugly bastard to the cops. Right, *boss?*"

Raising the blackjack he moved forward in Kowler's direction. HIs eyes were clamped on the man. As far as he was concerned, nobody else at all important to him was in the store. Using the blackjack on Kowler was the only thing that had to be done. Not a damn thing else made any difference to him.

Kowler took a step back, groped for the holster he carried and whipped out the gleaming black Thunderbolt. He aimed the gun at Ziggy. No man could possibly have missed a target at this range.

Ziggy was so crazed with anger it didn't stop him. He moved in the same direction as before, raising the hand with the blackjack as he came on. He was walking faster.

Kowler fired.

A gash flamed on Ziggy's cheek. The shot had scored without doing as much damage as Kowler must have figured on.

Ziggy sent the blackjack crashing down, but missed his target by inches. Kowler had moved further back, firing as he went. He was aiming more carefully and glancing behind him to make sure there weren't any obstructions in his way.

As he swerved right in order to avoid the customer counter at his back, Ziggy blocked him and lumbered forward with steps as heavy as if there were an extra weight on each leg. Ziggy's mouth had been widened hideously by the bullet-made streak, and a jagged red line on the coat showed where a chest wound must have been spouting blood.

Kowler wouldn't step backwards against the trap that the customer counter had turned into. Frantically he pulled the trigger of his gun, clicking it on six empty chambers. Ziggy was close enough to work the blackjack, which grazed Kowler's left cheek and then hit a shoulder. Kowler used all his strength to crash his gun against the bridge of Ziggy's nose.

It caught Ziggy. He stood swaying, and blood dripped out of his opened mouth. A growl oozed from his throat as he dropped down slowly to the floor.

Kowler took one glance at Jessup's implacable frozen gray face, then turned and ran out the door to the back entrance.

I snapped at Jessup, "I know what his car looks like. I'll drive yours."

Jessup nodded, the first movement he'd made in the thirty seconds or so since the mayhem had taken place. He hadn't been fast enough to interfere, but though he started moving after I did he joined me only half a minute after I got into the Plymouth across the street.

"Let him drive," Jessup ordered. "Savage is a stunt man and he might get the guy."

A cop started to protest, "But, Lieutenant —"

"I've thought it over and that's how I'm going to have it done. Shut up and let him drive."

The motor warmed to life under me. I didn't take the time to listen attentively, but I hoped that the car was in good shape. Any faults could make the difference to a try at catching up with Kowler, and might finish me as well as the five men in this car with me.

In my hurry I sped around the block to Essex Street, gauging the car for reactions and giving it my temporary approval. Kowler's Cad was pushing along Essex Street near the Jacob H. Schiff Parkway. I nodded to myself, relieved that I didn't have any further excuse for going easy on this car, and leaned forward for a chase. Kowler picked up speed when he realized I was on his trail, and did his best to shake me off. He streaked down Essex to East Broadway, where it led into Park Row, twisted into Fulton and then tried losing me on the MIller Highway. After turning off abruptly at Vestry, he followed Hudson Street to West Houston and Seventh, then zigzagged to Christopher.

"Son of a bitch," Jessup swore as I followed back to the highway, just making it on two wheels. "Kowler killed Ziggy, you know. I stayed behind to make sure that the creep was dead."

"Tough," I got out, "for Ziggy."

"Kowler's off his nut completely, now. Liable to do anything. He's in a panic. You'd think he would know he could probably get away with a plea of self-defense and some time upstate, that's all."

"Animals don't like to be put in cages," I said. "He's more animal than anybody I've ever seen."

Kowler turned off the Highway after it merged into Twelfth and drove down Thirty-fourth, taking Galvin to Forty-second, then following Tenth Avenue into Amsterdam.

I put on a burst of speed, checking the gas tank. There was just over a gallon. Good enough. You don't try to stunt in a car with much more than a gallon of gas in it. If something goes wrong, you'll find large and thick flames all around you. It doesn't take much brainpower to figure that out, but I've known stunting drivers to forget it till the last moment. What I had in mind would have to be done quickly and perfectly. There'd be no second chances in this league, no wait-till-next-year. One crack at it was all I'd get. Fervently I wished I was wearing a safety belt, the way I did at work.

"Put your heads in your hands," I called out, "and don't get tensed up, whatever you do. It's important to you."

Jessup warned, "You're not going to hurt him, for God's sake!"

"Do you want him or don't you?"

"Sure, but not in pieces."

"Take him any way you can, that's my advice."

"Look here, Savage, he's got rights the same as you have."

"This is one hell of a time for talking about rights! Either you get him any way you can or he goes free and he'll do whatever other damage pops into his twisted brain. Take your pick."

"I want him," Jessup said grimly, making up his mind. "He's a crazy goddamn wild animal. Get him."

I nodded and made my moves. Hooking both thumbs inside the wheel and keeping my hands at the five o'clock position, I turned to the right and dropped in my seat at the split second of the impact of the Plymouth into that Cad's back.

It worked exactly the way I'd figured, the left front of this car cracking into the right rear of the Cad and forcing it to swerve. There was a hideous screech of tires and a crash of breaking glass. The Cad shuddered.

Quickly I opened the door on my side, then ran out and came around to the Cad's front. That was when I stopped running. It wasn't necessary any more.

Kowler hadn't moved, or rather he'd done too much moving at the wrong time. He'd been taken completely by surprise and he'd paid for that. His head had crashed through the windshield. Blood coursed out of his neck as I watched. Frantically he tried to get out of the trap he was in, not realizing or caring how much more harm the motion would do him. He whined once, then closed his eyes and suddenly relaxed completely.

Two of the four patrolmen who had joined me looked away and went to work keeping the crowd near us from getting too close. A third man worked his way to the call box on Cathedral Parkway. The fourth cop stayed next to Jessup, who made sure that Kowler was dead before turning to me.

"Well, you did it."

"Got him you mean, Lieutenant. One way or the other I got him."

"The way you wanted," Jessup said flatly. He folded both hands on his big belly and looked patiently at me. "You were out to kill him."

"It was the fastest way."

"You had been watching him drive and, because you're a stunt man, you knew he was pretty bad in a crisis behind the wheel. He was likely to react the same way that nine drivers out of ten do: he'd get all tightened up and fight whatever happens and get killed fighting. That's exactly how it worked out."

"If it's a crime to guess," I snapped, "put the cuffs on me."

"I'd do it with any kind of a case," Jessup said gravely. "Besides, you're the one who panicked Kowler in the first place. You must have heard Ziggy in the back of that store, and then you started to work on Kowler to get him to sell out Ziggy."

"Kowler had it coming and so did Ziggy," I said. "Don't expect me to feel sorry for either of them."

"But you couldn't wait for the law to get to work. Justice is a lot too slow for the likes of you."

"In Kowler's case and Ziggy's, a sentence would probably have been a slap on the wrist. A year or two upstate somewhere, after years of appeals, and they'd be back in business as usual. This way you're rid of those two bums for all time."

"That's a good excuse for taking the law into your own hands." Jessup's fat face glowed in light from the nearest lampposts. "The punishment doesn't fit the crime."

"Kowler punished a lot of people who'd never hurt him," I said vehemently. "He twisted and destroyed lives, helped to make perverts that much sicker and did at least one murder that we know of. Maybe more. If you ever take his business apart, I bet you'll find that he was involved up to his neck in God knows how many sickening deals."

"Even if that's true," Jessup rumbled, "it doesn't mean . . ."

"I never thought I'd find a guy on the police brass with so much respect for scum like Kowler."

"Not for him, Savage, for the law."

"All right, I've got respect for the law, too. And for people. I don't go along with giving the Kowler types a good break because they had hard childhoods or their mothers were drunks. They had some chances to grow up into decent people and turned their backs on all of them. They purposely became what they did, and loved every minute of it. They get a boot out of their evil. It makes them happy. They can't be changed or reformed, not any more. It's too late for that. A quick death for them is a mercy for the rest of us."

Jessup shrugged. "All I can tell you, Savage, is that I wouldn't want to have your conscience."

I leaned forward intently. "Lieutenant, I wouldn't trade it for yours if you got down on your knees and begged. Take my word for that."

## NINETEEN

I was reading the clauses of the twenty-five cent insurance policy I had taken out while waiting for the midnight flight to be called at Idlewild, when I heard myself being paged.

Ever since I was allowed to take out insurance coverage, I've become a little hipped on the subject of policies, their clauses and indemnities. One time I was able to help a buddy of mine on account of that. He had hurt himself on a stunt, jumping three stories out of a window made of candy, and he was due for a hospital stretch. The movie we were both working on was being shot on the Missouri side of the Missouri-Kansas border; and I knew that the insurance laws in Kansas were more favorable. Against my buddy's will at the time I took him over the border and set up the story so he could claim he'd crashed in Kansas. He got a fine settlement out of the company and he was glad I'd done it, but we had a small argument about something else later on and he told me he wished to hell I could leave *something* alone just once.

An hour had passed since the wild ride that had finished Kowler. Besides making plane reservations in that time, I had kept myself busy on the long distance phone to Lore at Maria Gomez's place in Brentwood.

"You don't have to worry about the stag movie any more," I told her. "That part of it is all cleaned up by now, and it was about time."

"Oh yes, the — that movie."

"What's more, it looks like the Goodell killing is wrapped up, too," I said. "The lieutenant on the case is sure that one of the hoods did it and the hoods are in no condition to change the cop's mind. I tried to make it happen like that."

She laughed gratingly. "And you think the whole hellish business is over with?"

"Sure it is. What's wrong, Lore? Can't you believe you've been let off so lightly? Well, I'll bring you newspaper stories to prove it and I'll tell you a lot more than I want to say over the phone. I'll be there as soon as possible."

I had hung up ruefully. My hurry to get out there meant that I'd have to keep Rex at the New York kennel till my next trip out here on my want to a stunt job in Vermont . . .

I walked to the information desk in the airport waiting room to find out who had paged me. She was standing a little way off from the desk, a gaily wrapped package in one hard, workworn old hand, and wearing the same Sunday-best outfit as when she'd come to see me and catapulted me into the whole sordid mess. It was Lynne Darling, the floor maid at Lore's hotel.

"I was so afraid I'd miss you, Mr. Savage," she began excitedly as she came towards me with mincing little steps. "As soon as I heard over the radio that you'd killed all those gangsters or whatever it was, I tried to find you, but you'd left your hotel. That policeman who was with you, he told me where you'd be, so I came down here."

"It's nice to see you again, Lynne. I hope there's nothing else wrong."

"Oh no, everything's wonderful. That five hundred dollars you got for me is in my bank account and I — well, I wanted to show you how grateful I am."

She held out the gaily wrapped package toward me. I took it gingerly, hoping it wasn't anything expensive. I didn't want her spending any big chunk out of the money I'd stung Harold Radfield for. I felt a little better about that as soon as I had fumbled with the wrapping and opened the cardboard box inside. She'd bought me a portable movie camera, of all things, a good looking Brownie 8 with a fixed focus f/2.7 lens, an exposure dial for f-stop numbers and a threaded socket on top of it for the Brownie 8 movie light. It looked efficient as hell.

"A darn nice camera," I said honestly. "I'm glad to have it."

"The very least a Christian woman can do is to show she appreciates what somebody did for her," Lynne beamed. "I know it sounds like taking coals to Newcastle, you being in the real movies and all, but I've been told by somebody who ought to know that a lot of people in your business don't get around to buying cameras for themselves. I hoped it was something you didn't have."

"You called it right as far as I'm concerned," I lied as heartily as I could. "I've always wanted one. By the way, just out of curiosity, who is this person who ought to know and told you about movie people generally not having private cameras?

Who is it?"

"An actress, as a matter of fact," Lynne said. "I saw her with one of them only a day or so before coming to talk with you. She was mighty interested in cameras, how they worked and so on. She's the one who told me about it, a Spanish girl. Or Mexican. I don't know which."

"Would her name be Gomez, by any chance? Maria Gomez? Claims she has a rough time because she isn't American?"

"Yes, that's right. An awfully good actress, I've heard, but all she ever plays in is those 'b' pictures about horrible kids in high school. It bothers her a lot that she never gets a chance to do anything else, with all her talent and after the years she studied. She curses the Hollywood directors and producers, and calls them stupid, short-sighted pigs who give the good parts to North American women with blonde or red hair and a different accent from hers. Yes, I've heard a lot from Miss Gomez about her hardships."

I changed the subject away from Maria Gomez's familiar frustrations, but the other part of what had been said lingered unpleasantly. It bothered me that Maria should have taken a sudden interest in movie cameras. Worst of all, there was no reason I knew to be upset about it. But I couldn't get rid of the sudden conviction that the sooner I got Loré away from Maria's house, the better. I knew I wasn't going to reach L.A. again fast enough to suit me.

## TWENTY

A cab drove me from the airport to the winding driveway lined with silk oak trees that shimmered in the late morning sun on the way to Maria Gomez's house. The place gleamed brightly, too, in the shank of the morning.

After paying the cabbie I walked across the oval to the white frame brick house and rang the doorbell. I waited. The smell of clipped grass was strong. My watched showed eleven twenty-five — no, six, now. I rang twice more. The shadows had changed position very slightly by the time I knocked.

I was on the point of trying the door when it opened abruptly on Maria. I had never seen her looking better. She might have been poured into the soft shirtwaist dress of brown-and-black printed bamboo silk with its narrow pleats and bloused top. Her color was high. Excitement made her heart-shaped face gleam and widened the thrust of her breasts.

"Oh, it is you, *chico*. To what do I owe the pleasure of this visit — that is how you say, yes?"

"It's not you I'm visiting."

"Not me at all, *chico*? Not even a little bit?"

"You may not have known it, but the name is Mark."

184

"You seem very unfriendly now. And you want to see — ah, would it be Raymond?"

"I've no interest at all in your blond boy friend, and I'm not here to play games, Mary Gomer. And how are things back in Boston, where you hail from originally?"

"I do not understand," she said too quickly, and added in a rush, "Is it Lore you wish to see? I was afraid of this. It is awkward, in a way."

"You'd better explain that."

She sighed. "Come in, *chic —* . . ." A wicked gleam showed in her eyes. "No, *Mock*. That is the name, yes? Come in, *Mock*."

She led the way into the tropical-style living room I remembered from last time as having everything but mosquito netting and a place for pith helmets. Briskly she gestured me to sit down on the uncomfortable looking shepherd's chair, lit a cigarette in a long black holder after snapping the lighter irritably half a dozen times, and inhaled deeply before looking at me again. She glared at me on seeing that I hadn't sat down. Tautness was written all over her.

"You are making this difficult for me, *Mock*."

"What are you talking about? Either I see her or I don't. There's no sweat in that."

"It is not easy to tell you what I mean. You will be disappointed. You may think of Lore as being one sort of girl, but she is actually something different altogether. The discovery is certain to be as painful to you as it was to me. It is hard to know what I should say."

"You'll have to explain that to me, too. I guess I'm just not hearing straight, today."

185

"Lore is very wise in the ways of men, *chico*. She knows what kind of woman they want and how to be like that. Another woman can tell this when she sees Lore with a man to whom she is attracted. Lore has been flaunting herself for days now at my butler."

"What?"

"It is true. She and Raymond have been together many times in the last few days, I believe. I cannot prove it. If I could — *madre de Dios!* what a scene I would make them. But without proof I have to keep the promise I gave, that I would help Lore. After this trouble is over, I will not speak to her again or ever see her if I can help it. On that much, *chico*, I have decided."

"What kind of crap are you handing me?"

"*Chico*, I tell the truth."

"If that's the case, I'd hate to hear you lying," I snapped. "Now, where's Lore?"

"But *chico*, you must believe . . ."

I looked around angrily. Square-in-a-square carving on the door at the far end reminded me that it was the way to the bedroom where I'd seen Lore the last time I'd been at this place. I turned abruptly on my heels, pounded across to it, and just about wrenched the knob off as I charged into the bedroom.

And almost wished I hadn't.

There are some sights that a man instantly knows he'll never forget. They'll be triggered back into memory years later by a look, a word, or even a speech inflection. I knew right then that the sight of Lore in this garishly lit wine-red bedroom was

186

one of the moments I'd remember always.

Lore was nude, and harsh lights trapped the ivory whiteness of her flesh, the delicate perfection of breasts, the graceful slimness of hips, the smooth length of leg. That taut body was a work of art.

She lay on her back in the wide bed as if frozen. Her big eyes stared unblinkingly ahead. Her fists were clenched tightly. Even two chubby teardrops were in a state of suspended animation, hesitating on the curves of her cheeks. Not only was Lore Wylie uncovered, but she didn't seem to have heard a stranger coming into this room. Somebody took a step at the other end of the room and I realized that Lore hadn't been here by herself when I'd walked in.

The man I had last seen in a male bikini, blond muscular Raymond, was standing next to the bamboo blind over the window. He wore a dark blue bathrobe opened at the chest to show tufts of curly blond hair. The lower split showed a smooth down of blond hair glowing against the firm bared triangle of suntanned thigh.

I dredged up my vocal chords from somewhere deep in my kidneys. "What's going on here?"

Back of me Maria said calmly, "I told you, *chico*, but you did not believe."

Quickly I half-turned around to glance at the unnaturally calm Maria, and to the unusually self-effacing Raymond, then to a Lore Wylie who didn't seem to give a damn how many men saw her in the buff.

"Lore!" I said sharply. "What goes on?"

A look of terror flicked across Lore's eyes and

vanished. Fresh teardrops darted out of the corners of her eyes as she turned back into the taut, rigid, stone-like woman I'd already seen. Her lips clamped shut. I whirled around once again.

"How about you, Raymond? What are you up to? Did you get so sick of Maria's calling you a Yankee pig that you're after somebody else?"

"That's it," Raymond said thinly. There was contempt for me in his lidded eyes and in the crinkled lips. He was getting a boot out of this. "Did you think Lore Wylie isn't human? She's just like any other broad. Offer her what she really wants and she does what comes naturally. I made my offer the right way, that's all."

"I want to hear her say it." I turned back. "Is that true, Lore? Is it?"

"I — I yes." The voice belonged to an old, old woman trapped at the bottom of a well. "If they say it's true, it is."

"You're going to bed with Raymond?"

"Yes."

"Is it what you want to do?"

"Yes." She swallowed. "Please go away and leave me — us — alone."

"I don't believe it, Lore. Damn it, I couldn't possibly let this go on. A woman as scared as you are right now isn't set for a roll in the hay. Something's wrong here, and I'm damn well going to find out what."

"Nothing's wrong."

"The hell with that stuff! Get dressed, Lore. I'm taking you out of here, for a start."

"That is not true, *chico*," Maria Gomez said very softly from behind me.

188

I stiffened as I suddenly felt a cold cutting edge poised at the back of my neck just above the collarbone.

. "With this knife, *chico*," Maria added, "I will puncture you all over the body if you will not do exactly what I say. That is clear, yes?"

I cursed under my breath.

"For a start, *chico*, put your hands in front of you. Stretch them out as if you want to reach as far in front of you as possible."

I hesitated briefly, but remembered that Maria Gomez alias Mary Gomer hadn't made an empty threat since I'd known her, and she wouldn't have any trouble just planting that sticker of hers deep inside the back of my neck. She could manage it if I so much as started to make a wrong move.

I put my hands in front of me.

"Good," she said, approving the fact that I was so easy to get along with. "*Ramon! La silla!*"

I heard Raymond moving around lightly. When he halted, there was pressure against the backs of my knees.

"Sit down very slow," Maria ordered me. "Any extra motion you make, *chico*, you will regret."

I began sitting down very slow, the knife remaining at my neck. After moving a couple of inches I waited long enough to be sure that the knife hadn't put a hole in me, then repeated the process. As soon as my rear end touched the chair I sat back normally, damning all caution.

"You are a brave man, *chico*," she said, pulling the knife back. "But all brave men are stupid."

"Cut out the lectures," I snapped.

"Very good." In a louder voice she asked, "You

brought the clothesline rope, Raymond? Good. *Muy bueno.* Now use it!"

"You!" Raymond barked. "Put your hands at your sides."

Raymond tied me down as efficiently as any studio technician getting me ready for a stunt. The finished job didn't give me any chance to move around unless I dragged the chair with me, and Raymond got that effect without cutting my circulation off. There was a gloating devilment in Maria's face as she looked at me in this position. A low laugh rumbled deep in her throat.

I asked with controlled quiet, "What in hell is the point, Maria? Do you wnat me to see everything Raymond does to her?"

"Of course, *chico.* I want you to see it happen, all of it. You will see what your beautiful redhead," she nearly spat out that last word, "really is like in bed. How good she is to a lover. How obliging, how quick and willing to do all the things she is asked to , the beautiful redhead."

"You've lost your mind!"

"No, *chico,* not that. I am — how is it said? — impulsive, but I have not lost my mind."

"You must hate Lore Wylie because she's been more successful than you have."

"Yes, yes, *chico.*" She nodded tautly. "Lore gets the good parts because she is blond and fair and *yanqui,* and does not have to go to bed with people who can be good to her in the business. I have to sleep with fat old men so I can get parts in cheap pictures, and all because I am dark and *Latino.* Of course I hate her."

I blinked in surprise, taken aback by the

workings of such a viciously flighty mind. I've seen all sorts of criminals whose motives sounded like hers; but I hadn't expected to meet another "impulsive" one at the end of this trail. "You hate somebody, and that's enough reason to destroy her."

"Yes, *chico*, that is enough." She smiled grimly and turned. "We have wasted too much time."

Lore looked hypnotized, a small bird watching a huge and venomous snake. Why did she submit to something she loathed so much? Only one possible answer made any sense at all: there had to be blackmail in it.

Yes, it was pretty easy to figure out now. Maria must have said she'd give the whole story anonymously to the newspapers and pointed out that Lore would be up against a sex scandal and murder charge. Lore's deep-rooted sex fears hadn't let her believe a single word I'd been in such a rush to tell her over the phone about her being absolutely safe. She must have thought I was trying to be cheerful.

I turned to her. "Lore, don't go through with it and get yourself involved any deeper."

Lore, white-faced with shame, didn't answer.

"But she is eager to do this with Raymond, *chico*," Maria said, noisily retracting the knife edge back into the hollow of its handle. "Lore will enjoy it."

"But not as much as you will," I said crisply. "I've had the whole story pretty much straight since I got on the plane home a few hours ago. You couldn't think of any better way to ruin Lore Wylie than by forcing her to act in a very profitable stag movie. You knew about a guy who needed money desperately, so you and Robert Goodell got together on this venture, this business proposition."

"I do not deny what you say," she told me, still smiling. "It does not bother me any more if you know this."

"Because I'm a stunt man I also know that you and Goodell couldn't use a girl who looks like Lore, but you needed Lore herself. From that it follows what kind of a scheme you two cooked up. Goodell sent Lore a composition photograph that was obscene, and in which her face was superimposed on the real model's face. Lore flipped at the idea of any scandal at all. She lost her hold on reality as soon as she saw that, and was too damn upset to realize how much of a phony it was. She became so upset she tried to kill herself."

"Most of this you knew before," Maria said quietly. "How much more do you know now?"

"I'll get to that. Goodell phoned Lore at the hospital soon after he heard what had happened. He said that he had something to tell her about the photograph and a stag movie. Lore went to see him. She was told that if she hopped into bed with Goodell, she'd be given a chance to buy the movie. Goodell made it sound as if the idea had just come into his head, but actually it would have to be his major point. Before the girl arrived, he'd have secretly arranged for a noiseless movie camera to take pictures of what happened between them, and probably use infra-red lighting in the room. That's how he was going to get the actual movie, by blackmailing her into doing those things that

192

would be in the movie when it was made in the apartment. A damn good idea, I must say, and it might have worked out with some other woman, but it didn't work out with this one."

"So what, *chico?*"

"So there's never been a movie for you to ruin Lore with," I said, "and there never could be. Isn't that too goddamn bad!"

"I am not worried, *chico.*" Maria reached around for something out of my sight and slowly came back into view again. I stared at the small but efficient gray thing that was in her hands now. She made a point of showing it to me in the garish light, smiling as she did it.

Maria Gomez was holding a portable movie camera.

## TWENTY-ONE

"You see, *chico?*" she grinned. "When one idea will not work on account of stupidity or incompetence — and Goody was not smart enough to do anything well except photographing pictures — then another idea *will* work. There'll be a stag movie of Lore after all, and I am going to direct it and make the pictures myself right now."

Lore suddenly gasped, shock widening her eyes as she stared down at nudity and hurriedly pulled the quilt up around her. She was behaving like a human being in trouble, though, and not like a stone statue.

"Oh God, I've been a fool," she whispered. "I'm so mixed up I can't think straight any more, but I've got to get away from here now. I've got to."

"No!" Maria called out, turning to Raymond. "You know what to do."

Raymond asked tonelessly, "Now, Maria?"

"Of course, stupid. We waited till this one, this admirer of hers, would come so he'd see with his own eyes. It may be more amusing if Lore does not seem to be cooperating."

Raymond nodded briefly, undoing the knot of his bathrobe and slipping it off. Muscles rippled down both arms as he gapped his flat stomach, gleaming balefully in what must have been infra-red light. A row of goose pimples appeared on his wide shoulders when he skirted the white-topped dining table some fifteen feet from the bed and started to walk over to Lore.

Maria chuckled and sighted the camera so that she'd be able to photograph what happened on the bed.

Lore Wylie watched out of frightened eyes that flicked desperately toward the door that was too far away, and back again. Desperation crimped the breath in her lungs.

"Lamp!" I called out. "Lamp on the night table! Get the lamp!"

Still staring at Raymond's advance, she reached out blindly for the dark table lamp, holding it in one hand as she waited.

As Raymond drew closer to where I was tied down, I raised myself slightly. At the first move I felt as if skin were being peeled off my body piece by piece. There wasn't enough room between my legs and the chair's front to hold an envelope. But I had been able to move around when tied to a chair for that movie stunt on the George Washington Bridge. If I remained still and simply let this happen, I knew I'd hate myself forever.

Practically numb by now, I pushed myself till I bumped into Raymond, the top of my head catching him just below the chin instead of against the neck. My numb anger had hurt the timing, though, and I hadn't hit him nearly as hard as I'd wanted to.

Raymond lurched briefly to one side, then grinned down at me in the chair. His right hand made a fist and as I moved forward clumsily his open left hand slapped my face and his right fist crashed into my side. I fell over, thunderously.

With a contemptuous little smile, Raymond stepped over the fallen chair that I was tied to. I pushed forward very quickly on the chance of tripping him down to my level, but he dodged me deftly and advanced to the bed.

I called out, "Hit the edge of the lamp off his skull, Lore!" The hollow and meaningless-sounding syllables tripped over each other as they tumbled out of my mouth. For my own satisfaction I added, "The bastard, the bastard, the son-of-a-bitching bastard!"

Painfully I forced myself to get up again in the chair. I needed several tries at lifting my weight plus the chair from a lying down position, and out of tiredness alone nearly tipped myself over on the other side.

I was on time to see Lore finally throw the lamp at Raymond. He made a motion with his hands to show that he was irritated by the distraction and moved forward, actually bringing himself into the lamp's orbit.

It caught Raymond high on the forehead, freezing him in one spot but loosening the fists, softening the back muscles and dropping the shoulders. As I watched, Raymond fell forward across the bed. The springs creaked, and Raymond's body slipped off the edge of the bed and down to the floor.

I called out to Lore, "Get this rope off me!"

She glanced down fearfully at the quilt with her unclothed body beneath.

"Dammit, hurry up!"

"But I . . ." she started to whimper.

"You want to get us both killed? You want to be found dead that way? You want your picture that way in every paper up and down California?"

She let out a little gasp and determinedly pushed the quilt away from herself, then stood up shakily and ran around to my back. As she fumbled hastily at one of the knots back of me, trying to help me at top speed, she tightened the pressure of the ropes around me. For a minute the room turned gray. I swivelled my head around in hopes that the activity would help me bear pain, and then almost forgot about the pain. I could see Maria Gomez put down the camera and grab her knife instead.

Maria started directly for Lore, but I moved the chair so that I was facing Maria instead and Lore was back of me working at the ropes.

Maria called out, "Get away from his, Lore."

The redhaired girl worked at my bonds. Maria aimed the knife at a point over my head and when the knife hand moved I ducked forward slightly and raised the chair. The knife caught a point in the chair that was directly beside my neck. Maria pulled the weapon out swiftly and raised it once again to stab at Lore from an area that would be out of my reach altogether.

I called out, "Duck, Lore!"

The knife whistled dully past me. For a split-second nothing happened at all, and then I felt Lore's fingers working persistently at the ropes.

Maria caught her balance and brandished the

**197**

knife once more. "If you do not get away from him and do it this minute, I will kill him."

Automatically I said, "Keep at it, Lore. Don't listen to her."

Maria raised the knife above my head, ready to carry out her threat. Something stirred on the floor and there was a sighing, wheezing sound that had to be coming out of a pair of human lungs.

Maria stepped back and turned to look at a point out of my sight now. She said viciously:

"So you have come back to us!"

"I couldn't help what happened," Raymond said slowly. "Let me get hold of that bitch now, and I'll really put the blocks to her."

"Get her, yes," Maria agreed vehemently. "But take care of this pig first."

She moved to one side and I turned in Raymond's direction. He was getting up slowly so he'd have a little more time to readjust himself. He swayed at his first heavy steps, then reached a hand up towards the vivid blue mark just above his left temple.

"There's no sense trying to get them ropes untied, baby," he growled to Lore. "I'll take care of your boy friend before you get even halfway finished. And then you'll do something else with me, baby."

"Stay there, Lore," I shouted. "Stay against the back of this chair."

Maria laughed.

"Don't pay attention to what anybody else says, Lore," I told her. "Don't move away from the back of the chair, that's all you have to do."

I couldn't tell if she did what I wanted or not.

All my energies were focused on what was happening in front of me.

Raymond grinned cruelly as he started towards me. He was all set to do some destroying now, I could tell, the more the better. His hands pantomimed strangling at every step closer that he took.

He halted three feet away.

"All right," he said heavily. "I'm going to smack you silly first, before I do anything else. I owe it to you for coaching her about throwing that lamp."

"Try it and see how far you get."

"I'll get where I want to."

"How come you're hesitating, if that's the case? If you're so damn sure of yourself, let's see some stuff."

"I've got a message for you first, wise guy. A little extra message. Frosting on the cake, you might call it."

"Well?"

He smiled as he leaned slightly forward. This was fun for him.

"I'm not going to knock you out completely, wise guy. Not all the way. Uh-uh. I want you to see each and every damn thing that I do with your girl friend after I take care of you. Got that?"

"I'm shivering, that's how scared I am."

I leaned forward, balancing myself on the balls of my feet as I waited tensely. When he made a move I made mine. I ducked my head down to one side and brought up the back of the chair as fast and hard as I could. My face thumped against his bronzed chest, and for a moment his heart hammered on my right ear. He reeled back, both hands around the front of his neck where he'd been hit. He fell so heavily that the floor shook, and his body settled as if for a long, long rest.

I called out, "Lore! Keep on with this!"

She was untying knots as quickly as she could when Maria came at me again. The woman walked warily this time, very slowly. As she turned the knife in her right hand, the steel blade gleamed.

Waiting till she was three feet away, I suddenly jumped at her. I couldn't get far, of course; but the move did catch her off-guard. Now that she had picked up a healthy respect for me, she took a startled step backwards — and tripped over Raymond's unconscious body.

I allowed myself a small gratified nod that the first part of my impromptu plan had worked out. The rest of it had to be handled quickly.

After hopping the few steps to Raymond's side, I let myself trip across him in a fall, relaxing the muscles as I did it in order to keep from being maimed by the chair.

I made it by inches, taking pleasure in kicking one of Raymond's thighs at the moment of landing in order to push myself to Maria Gomez's side. I made it at a ninety-degree angle and propelled myself further with bruised arms. My head briefly and unsatisfyingly touched Maria's pulsing left breast, but I didn't halt till my shoulders pinned her down to the floor.

Maria cursed in Spanish and English, and pulled back the knife for leverage. I used a woman's time-honored weapon, bending my head down and biting the knuckle of the right thumb. Maria gasped at the pain, and the knife dropped down to the floor at her far side.

"Pig! Pig!"

Her fists lashed my head and neck, shoulders and chest in blind uncalculated hatred. The writhing body under me moved the knife very slightly, still further beyond my reach.

Carefully I inched my head over to the side where she had left the glinting knife. My neck muscles stretched almost unbearably as I reached for it, darting my tongue out to force the knife back and closer to me. My upper teeth gripped an edge of the hilt, raising it. I allowed that edge to drop against my lower teeth and with tongue as a guard, moved slightly backwards to a more comfortable place. Then I set the opposite end of the knife against my upper teeth. By nibbling at it almost as if I was handling steely corn on the cob, I worked my mouth up till I had the hilt firmly between my teeth and the knifetip finally pointed downwards.

From one side of mouth I called, "Lore, take this and finish the job on these ropes."

"Don't need it," she said shortly.

"For God's sake," I began.

"Wait."

"That's what I've been doing all the time. For heaven's sake, get it over with!"

"I started to do it with my own hands and that's how it'll be done in — just — a — second." Her deft fingers moved once more across the ropes and she suddenly gave a deep-throated sigh of satisfaction. "It's all over now. All over."

I blinked confusedly. Clothesline rope was tumbling down around me. With a wary nod I realized that I had finally been untied in spite of Lore's original prudish reluctance to expose herself.

"Don't do anything else till you call the cops," I said. "That's the most important thing now."

Maria's eyes followed with fearful urgency as Lore's bare footsteps receded, then she looked anxiously at me.

"You can't do this," she got out, the accent fading for the first time since I'd known her. "Not the police."

"Just you watch," I said, adding mockingly, "*chiquita.*"

"The cops will ruin me," she said quickly. "My whole career will be smashed to pieces and I'll be on the rocks for good and all."

"That isn't unfair, considering what you tried doing to Lore — and what you actually did to Goodell. You got so mad at Goodell when he fluffed the chance to degrade Lore Wylie for all time that you took the knife Lore had used and you killed him with it."

"*I* did? But I heard Lore confess to the murder."

"She admitted she stabbed Goodell three times. But that's not what happened, according to the Manhattan cops and what I saw myself. Goodell was stabbed about ten to fifteen times all over the body, Maria, like you said you'd stab me if I didn't do what you wanted."

I heard Lore's sudden intake of breath in the next room and added loudly, "I'd have told you last time I was here, but you wouldn't have believed me then and that might have made you feel worse. All you really cared about, Lore, was the stag mov — ..."

My breath almost caved in at the sudden rush of pain. Blood was once more trying to circulate vigorously in my numbed body and the change was as abrupt as if a weight had fallen on me. I'd have been in a stronger position for awhile if I had remained tied up.

"I promise I'll go away somewhere," Maria said urgently, too self-centered as usual to hear anybody else's distress, "if you don't call the police."

I looked at the *Latino* from Boston through mists of pain and remembered the cruelty with which she'd killed Robert Goodell because he hadn't done what Maria had grimly made up her mind that he had to do.

"There'd be other tricks you'd pull," I said heavily. "Even if I could let you get away, Maria, I'm pretty sure Lore would talk. There's no way in the world you could keep both of us quiet. You're all finished, Maria."

Pain must have been reflected in my face because she looked at me, then down at the ropes twisted on the floor, then up at me again. She understood what was happening inside my system to freeze me for a while.

Determination glinted in her eyes. She brought up both hands back of my head. I was too weak to twist away from the power she had. Then she forced my head down with all the pressure she could bring to it, down against her left breast where the knifepoint plunged deep. Blood was spounting as I tried to pull myself away.

But she was quicker. One of her hands fixed the knife immovably in place, drawing my lips tight together against the handle. I couldn't let go of it. My lips felt on fire and I didn't have enough strength to help myself. The other hand on the back of my head she pulled down again, inflicting one more knife wound on her body. Blood spurted, drenching me in it.

Her strength was fading. Pain flicked through me one more time when I rolled away from her, dropping the knife.

Maria's eyes glazed as I looked back at her. The twisted smile straightened, becoming prim and rigid as she died.

## TWENTY-TWO

The Boeing Intercontinental hit an air pocket when we were half an hour out of Burbank.

At my side Lore Wylie said, "It shouldn't take me more than a day or two to clear things up with the police in New York. I want to tell them the truth about what happened between me and Goodell."

"You don't have to," I said. "It'll take a hell of a lot of time and be pretty rough on you, to boot."

"Mark, I've been afraid of scandals my whole life long, but if I meet this head-on now, I won't be afraid any more. I won't ever think of slashing my wrists again. I'll know I can face anything else that ever happens to me. One thing I've learned after all this is simply that anticipating the worst is a lot more difficult than experiencing the worst."

"If you're free during the week," I said carefully, "we might run into each other. I've got a few days' work in New York."

They were shooting Westerns in New York that year, doing interiors at the Gold Medal Studios in the Bronx, and exteriors upstate around Woodstock. Hollywood producers get flat feet from following trends, but I didn't really mind this one because I've almost always been a sucker for travel.

"I'll pick up Rex from the kennel before I start to work," I said. "Be nice to see her again, now that everything's all right with me for a while — a short while, I hope."

"A lot of things are almost perfect for me, Mark. Jules Schlosser called before I left and wants me back to work for Globe, but I told him I'd rather free-lance. And Harry Radfield was foolish enough to call and ask if I'd like to hire him again as my business manager. I had the great pleasure of telling him to take a flying jump to the moon."

"You're very lucky if you've got everything you want."

"With one exception, Mark," she said slowly. "I've been curious about that for a long time, maybe for a shockingly long time. Something I've been missing in my life."

"Let me hear what it is, Lore."

"I've started to wonder how things could be if I was with a man I really felt strongly about. For a long time I've wondered if I'd ever meet a man who'd attract me so much. And I think I've met one. I hope so, Mark."

When we got back to her hotel a few nights later on a very pleasant date, and after time enough for her to get used to the idea of what we both knew was going to happen, we went up to Lore's room and I finally showed her what she'd been missing.

These days she tells me that she can't keep from wondering how she's ever going to make up for all the lost time. I've given her my word that I'll do all I can to help out.


**THE END**